Books by Ellen Howard

A CIRCLE OF GIVING
WHEN DAYLIGHT COMES
GILLYFLOWER

Gillyflower

Gillyflower

by ELLEN HOWARD

ATHENEUM · 1986 · NEW YORK

Atheneum
Macmillan Publishing Company
866 Third Avenue, New York, NY 10022

Composition by Heritage Printers, Charlotte, North Carolina
Printed and bound by Fairfield Graphics, Fairfield, Pennsylvania
Calligraphy on halftitle and title pages by Jeanyee Wong
Designed by Mary Ahern

10   9   8   7   6   5   4   3   2   1

Library of Congress Cataloging-in-Publication Data

Howard, Ellen.   Gillyflower.

SUMMARY: Sexually abused by her father and fearing
for the safety of her younger sister, Gilly seeks the
courage to tell someone what is happening.
[1. Child molesting—Fiction. 2. Incest—Fiction.
3. Fathers and daughters—Fiction] I. Title.
PZ7.H83274Gi   1986   [Fic]   86-3584
ISBN 0-689-31274-1

For all the Gillys.

The author is grateful to the following people for their help: Lucy Berliner, MSW, Coordinator of Child Research Projects, Sexual Assault Center, Harborview Medical Center, Seattle, Washington; Detective William T. Cross, Lake Oswego Police Department, Lake Oswego, Oregon; Dr. Henry Giaretto and the staff of the Institute for the Community As Extended Family, San Jose, California. Thanks are also due, for the second time, to the Magic Ending Fairy, Jane Yolen.

"... the fairest flowers o' the season
Are our ... streak'd gillyvors."

William Shakespeare
THE WINTER'S TALE

Gillyflower

CHAPTER ONE

E WERE UNDERNEATH the rhododendron bush, my sister Honey and me, the first time I heard their voices behind the hedge. They were laughing. That's what made me stop to listen. The laughter. It sounded happy . . . carefree.

"Don't stop," Honey said. "C'mon, Gilly. Finish the story."

I tried to think about the story I had been telling—something about Juliana, my made-up princess. Something about her faerie gown. "Uh, yeah" I said. "Her gown. It's all pearly pink and . . ."

"Like this?" Honey said, twirling the doll we had made from a twig and an upside-down blossom.

"Yeah, like that. That's right. When she dances, her gown whirls out around her legs, all pinky-silk and nice . . ."

The laughter stopped, but I could still hear a voice—not what it said, but just the way it sounded—smooth and warm and silky the way I imagined Juliana's gown.

"Gil-*ly*!" Honey whined.

But I didn't answer her. I was listening to the voice, to its rippling happiness. And then the voice laughed again, and I thought of the way Mar used to laugh when I was little, and it made a hard, hurting place in my stomach, and I had to close my eyes.

UNDER the rhododendron bush was my special place. I didn't share it with anyone but Honey.

"That rhododendron needs pruning," Mar had been saying ever since we moved into the house. But Mar never had time, and of course, Dad didn't do it, so it just kept getting bigger. "I'll bet that rhododendron has been grow-ing in this yard for fifty years," Mar would say.

"What rhododendron?" Dad would say, looking up from his book, his eyes unfocused.

"The *pink* rhododendron in the back yard," Mar would say, and I could hear the sharp edges in her voice. "If you ever did a little work around the yard, you'd know which rhododendron!"

And then they'd be off again, fighting, the words fly-ing back and forth harder and louder, until I slipped out the back door, covering my ears.

The rhododendron was a place to go where it was quiet. The leaves were big and shady green, and the criss-crossy branches arched so that, from the house, no one could see underneath. Hunkered down inside, on the smooth, grassless ground, I could look out and see every-thing, but no one could see me. I was safe.

It was under the rhododendron that I first imagined Juliana and first made a doll of her from the pink rhodo-

dendron blossoms. That was last spring, after Mar got her
job working evenings at the hospital, and Dad . . . Last
spring, when the secret began.

HONEY was tugging at my arm because I had stopped
telling the story again. "Gilly," she was saying. "Gilly!"

"Hush," I said. "Listen."

Honey got quiet, and her brown eyes got big, listening. "A lady," she said in a loud whisper. "I hear a lady
and some kids."

"Let's look," I said.

Where the rhododendron had grown up next to the
laurel hedge, the hedge didn't have any leaves on our side.
It made holes you could look through to see into the yard
of the house behind ours. Honey and I crawled around the
bush and peeked through.

"A lady," Honey whispered, so loudly I was afraid
they were going to hear us. Honey nodded her head sol-
emnly. "It's a lady all right! And two girls. Just like us."

"Shhh!" I was hissing at her, and all the time, I was
looking at those girls.

Honey was wrong. They weren't like us at all. Not
at all.

HONEY is my little sister. Well, really her name isn't
Honey. It's Beatrice. I'm the one who nicknamed her
Honey. It was when I was just a kid and didn't know any
better. They were calling her "Bea," and I thought they

meant "bee," like in "honeybee." It made sense to me then. In a way, it still does, because that's what she reminds me of—a brown-and-gold honeybee. She even, sort of, buzzes around—"busy as a bee," like Mar says.

But cute as she is, Honey isn't pretty, any more than I'm pretty. The girls in the yard behind the hedge were *pretty*—the rosy-cheeked, golden-curls kind of pretty you read about in books. They looked clean and neat and ... shining. Cared for. I liked the way the lady's hand rested, light and loving, on the bigger girl's shoulder. I liked the easy way they talked together, smiling and touching and ... leaning close.

I thought only Honey and I knew about the new neighbors, until I heard Mar telling Dad about them the next morning.

Dad looked up, kind of sharp. "Neighbors?" he said. "In that old, falling-down place? I figured it was ready for demolition like this dump."

"These old houses would be nice if they were fixed up," Mar said, kind of wistfully. "It's a couple with two kids. I'm glad. It'll be someone nearby for Gilly and Honey to play with."

Dad looked grouchy. "Gilly and Honey don't need anyone to play with," he said. "I liked the neighborhood the way it was. Quiet. Nobody bothering us."

I *DIDN'T* need anyone to play with. Ever since the secret began, I felt funny with other kids. I thought probably everyone in my new school could tell, just by looking at me. Anyway, nobody here seemed to like me much. I *didn't* need anyone. I had Honey, after all . . . and Juliana.

I liked playing with Honey. I liked telling her stories and taking care of her. "This is your baby sister. You can help take care of her." Mar told me when Honey was born, and I *did* take care of her. In fact, it was a good thing Honey had me, especially when Mar started working. Dad wasn't very good at taking care of kids. Most of the time, he was busy—reading or, once in a while, involved in a new job. Not that he didn't love us—in his way, as Mar said. He even started telling me so sometimes, after Mar got the job at the hospital.

"You're my own baby girl," Dad would say to me in the evening, when Mar was at work, and Honey was in bed. "I don't know what I'd do without my baby."

That was when he began to want me to stay up to keep him company. The light from the TV would flicker blue at the other end of the room, and he would hold me on his lap and hug me real tight against him. I liked the hugging. It was only the other stuff—the stuff that made me feel smothery and sick—that I didn't like.

"I won't hurt you," Dad would say. "I won't hurt my baby."

I was sure he didn't *mean* to hurt.

TIMES like those were when I most 'specially liked to close my eyes and think about Juliana.

Pretend I'm not me, I liked to think. Pretend I'm not Gilly Harper at all.

Pretend I'm someone good.

And pretty.

And happy.

Pretend I'm someone special.

Pretend . . . *I am Juliana. I am Juliana, dancing in a pearly pink gown that whirls and swirls around my legs. I am dancing beneath the flowering bush for all my kingdom to see.*

How beautiful she is! say the smiling people. How happy she is! How good!

And I swoop and swirl and lift and twirl—lost in the music that twinkles my toes. I am dancing!

I'm not Gilly. I don't want to be Gilly!

I am Juliana, dancing.

CHAPTER TWO

THIS AFTERNOON, after school, why don't you go over and meet those new girls," Mar said, bending to kiss me as I left for school that morning. I could see her eyes slide sideways to see what Dad would say, even as she kissed me. "Why don't you?" she said, and her voice was a little too loud.

Dad pretended he was reading, but I saw the way his eyebrows pulled together in a frowning black line.

"Take Honey with you, and go after school," Mar said. She handed me my lunch money. "Better get going, chicken. It's late. I'm going back to bed for a while," she said, more to the top of Dad's head, showing over the newspaper, than to me.

Dad grunted.

"Do you *have* to go to work today, Mar?" I said, not able to stop the words before they were out.

"You know I do, Gilly. Don't start that again."

I could hear the tiredness in her voice. Dad was between jobs right then, so of course Mar had to work, and the three-to-eleven shift was all she could get. She had explained it to me before when I begged her to stay home. "Your dad's right here if you need anything," she had said.

So now I said, "I'm sorry." I won't start that again, I

told myself, ashamed. "Have a good sleep, Mar," I said, and she smiled at me, kind of grateful, I thought.

"That's my girl," she said as I went out. She closed the door.

OF COURSE, I didn't go meet the new girls. Mar forgot all about it, as I thought she would.

I could feel the emptiness of the house when I opened the door that afternoon after school. I found Mar's note on the kitchen bulletin board.

Gilly —

Would you do a load of laundry? I've got to have some clean uniforms, and I didn't get them done before I had to leave for work.

Mrs. Corliss will bring Honey home from preschool.

Dad's at an interview.

Love,
Mar

I pushed some dirty dishes on the counter out of the way and put my books down. A pile of clothes was mounded on the floor beside the washer. I began to stuff them in, feeling sort of . . . comfortable, listening to the emptiness of the house.

At an interview. Dad was always having interviews. Sometimes, he even got a job. Trouble was, the jobs never lasted. "I don't have to take that off anyone," I would hear him telling Mar, or "I'm wasted in a dead-end job like that. I've got a master's degree, for chrissakes, a *master's* degree, and they expect me to sell junk!"

I finished loading the washer and pulled out the knob to make the water run in. I measured out the detergent and the powdered bleach, then wandered to the frig to see if there was anything to eat while I waited for the washer to fill. I found a little cheese, but that was all. I wondered what we would have for dinner, and whether I would have to fix it. Mar must have overslept again. She *could* have gone to the store, I thought.

The washer was chugging away at the clothes. Nibbling the chunk of cheese, I poured in first the detergent, then the bleach. The swirl of water and clothes gulped the bluish granules and spewed them out as bubbles. I closed the lid.

It would be awhile before the wash was done. I finished the cheese. I looked around the kitchen at the unwashed dishes in the sink, the clutter on the counters, and I thought I ought to clean up a little, but I didn't.

Instead I went out the back door to the rhododendron bush.

THEY were out there, just as I had hoped they would be—the girls and their mother. I watched them through the hedge. Mary Rose was wearing a yellow sweatshirt that looked brand new.

Mary Rose Gibbs. That was how Miss Gates, our teacher, had introduced her. "This is Mary Rose Gibbs, students. She has transferred to our school from Forestville."

Mary Rose had stood up at her seat and turned around and smiled. She didn't blush or anything. *I* would have sunk right through the floor!

From my desk in the very back corner, I had watched Mary Rose all day. For a new girl, she sure didn't act nervous, and I figured she was smart because when Miss Gates asked questions, she often knew the answers and put up her hand. Of course, I usually knew the answers too, but I never put up my hand any more. Only once in a while, I *had* to answer because Miss Gates told me to, and then she usually said, "Speak up, Gillian, so we all can hear you." And then everybody looked at me, and I wished I could disappear in a puff of smoke the way I imagined Juliana could with her crown of invisibility.

Now, through the hedge, I watched Mary Rose's mother haul a big plastic trash can out of their ramshackle shed. Their yard was littered with rusty tin cans and disintegrating papers the way yards get when no one lives in a house for a long, long time.

"Let's see who can clean up her section first," I heard Mrs. Gibbs say. "It will go faster if we make a game of it. Mary Rose, you pick up around the shed. I'll do the lawn. And Daphne, you can clean up the flower beds."

Daphne. *That* was the big girl's name. I had never

heard that name before. I tried to picture how to spell it. I thought it *sounded* beautiful. Not like my dumb name. Gillian. No one ever knew how to say it, if they saw it written. "Gill," I had to say, "like 'Jack and Jill went up the hill.'" A dumb name! But "Daphne" and "Mary Rose" were pretty. As pretty as the girls themselves. As pretty as Juliana's name, which I found in a book.

Daphne was pulling at a twisted piece of metal wedged in the low branches of a bush. She yanked so hard she fell over backwards when it came free. Mrs. Gibbs and Mary Rose laughed, and I laughed too. Daphne laughed when she got over her surprise.

Mrs. Gibbs.

Daphne.

Mary Rose.

"Gilly! Gilly! Where are you?" It was Honey, home from preschool.

"Gilly?" I could see her standing on the back stoop, clutching the edge of the screen door. Her voice sounded small and a little scared, but I didn't want to answer. I wanted her to go away and leave me alone with Mary Rose and her family.

"Gil-ly!" I could hear the growing panic in Honey's voice. The Gibbses could probably hear her, too. They'd be wondering why someone didn't take care of that little kid, crying on their neighbor's back stoop.

I crawled out from underneath the rhododendron

bush and stood up, brushing the dirt off my knees. *Some-one* had to take care of her. And it seemed like that some-one was always me.

THAT WEEK, and all the next, while the sunshine held, I watched Mary Rose through the hedge whenever I could.

"Lemme watch too, Gilly," Honey would beg. "I wanna watch, too."

"Only if you're still as a mouse," I would say.

"I will. I will. Still as a mouse." Honey would nod her head in big up-and-down swoops, her eyes round and serious.

"We don't want them to know we're watching," I told her.

"No-o-o," said Honey. "No, no, no. Why not, Gilly? Why don't we want them to know?"

"Just because," I said.

Mary Rose and Daphne and Mrs. Gibbs cleaned up their yard. They pulled weeds out of the flowerbeds and clipped the bushes into tidy shapes. On the weekend, a tall, yellow-haired man joined them. He mowed down the weeds and the long, flopped-over grass until the lawn was smooth and short and patchy yellow. Then they scattered some powdery stuff all over, and Daphne and Mary Rose took turns watering it in with a long green hose. The man cut sharp edges all the way around the lawn with a shovel, so the grass didn't straggle off into the flower beds. Then he dug up the beds, turning the dirt over in moist, brown chunks. Mrs. Gibbs clipped the grass away from the edges of the red tile stepping stones the mowing had uncovered in the grass.

"Look, Gordon," she called when she was working on her hands and knees in a corner of the yard. "Look at these coral bells coming up! There's quince flowering by the shed, and camellias under the bedroom window. Isn't this a wonderful yard?"

"Daddy, when can we plant *our* flowers?" I heard Daphne ask.

"Oh, isn't it going to be beautiful?" Mrs. Gibbs said.

"Yuck," said Mary Rose. "I dug up a worm!"

CHAPTER THREE

HE NEXT WEEKEND, it rained. When I woke on Saturday morning, I heard the gurgle of rain in the gutter above our bedroom window, and my heart went thud.

The Gibbses were going to plant their summer flowers that weekend. I had heard them say so. But even if they planted in the rain, I knew Mar wouldn't let me go outdoors to watch. I was sick so much last winter, the doctor told Mar I'd have to have my tonsils out if I got sick again.

I lay in bed with my eyes open and listened to the rain tapping against the window and to Honey's buzzing little snore beside me, and I felt sad. I wondered about the flowers the Gibbses had been going to plant. I tried to imagine how their yard would look when summertime came.

Like a kingdom of flowers, I thought. *Everything tidy and cared for, brilliant with colors and scents. A kingdom of beauty for queens and princesses, a kingdom of flowers to dance in,* I thought. *A kingdom of flowers to dance in . . .*

"Gilly," I heard Dad whisper through the silently opened crack of the bedroom door. "Gilly, get up and keep me company."

I squinched my eyes shut and lay very still. Go away, I prayed. Please, go away.

"Gilly, get up. Your mother's asleep, and I'm lonesome, all by myself," Dad whispered, a little more loudly. The whisper sounded sad.

I knew I should get up.

But I couldn't move. My breath stopped, and the smothery feeling began to close over me. I tried to think about Juliana, Juliana dancing in her flowers. I tried to hear her music, drowning out the whisper.

"Sid?" It was Mar's voice, sleepy, calling from their room. "What's the matter, Sid?"

Quietly, the door clicked shut.

I let go my breath in shaky gasps. My heart was pounding hard.

"HI, aren't you the girl who lives around the corner?"

It was Monday, and I was walking home from school. I put my umbrella down in front of my face and walked faster, keeping my eyes on the sidewalk.

"Hey, didn't you hear me? I said, aren't you the girl who lives in the house around the corner?" Mary Rose's voice spoke from behind me. I could hear her rubber boots, sloshing through the puddles.

My heart was lurching, funny, against my ribs—sort of thump, thump, thump, real fast, and then it would miss a beat.

"Hey! Wait up!" Mary Rose yelled, and because I didn't know what else to do, I did.

Her umbrella bumped against mine, sending a little shower of raindrops splashing into my face.

"I'm sorry." She laughed. "I thought you didn't hear me. *Aren't* you the girl around the corner?"

I nodded, keeping my eyes on the gleaming wet sidewalk.

"I thought so," she said. "Hi, my name is Mary Rose. I think we're in the same class."

"I know," I said. I could feel her peering around under our umbrellas to see my face.

"I'm sorry, I don't know *your* name yet," she said.

"Gillian." I thought my voice sounded squeaky. I cleared my throat. "Gillian Harper," I said.

"Glad to meet you, Gillian."

We were almost at the corner. I looked across the street at my house, second from the end of the block. It looked rundown and sad, standing in the middle of our dripping, weedy yard. My heart turned when I saw Dad standing in the doorway, looking out through the rain.

"Hey, this is great," Mary Rose said. "Living so close together. Want to walk to school with me tomorrow?"

"I gotta go," I said. I splashed into the stream of rainwater flowing next to the curb and almost ran across the street.

"Wait," I heard her say. "Want to meet here, at the corner?"

"OK," I said desperately. Maybe he's not watching for *me*, I thought. Maybe he doesn't even see me coming.

"Great! See you tomorrow. Gillian?" I could hear the puzzlement in her voice when I didn't answer her.

"Who was *that*?" Dad said as I came up on the porch, shaking the water off my umbrella. He held the door open.

"Just a girl from school," I said.

"Well, I don't like her looks. Remember, you've got your sister to take care of after school. You can't run off playing with other kids. You've got responsibilities here at home."

"I know." I headed toward the bathroom to put my umbrella in the tub to drip.

"Just so you do," I heard Dad say, stomping his feet as he went into the kitchen. A minute later, I heard him slam the refrigerator door.

"THE BEAST locked Juliana in the tower and wouldn't let her come out," I told Honey that night, making up her bedtime story as I went along.

"Was it 'cause she was bad?" Honey asked.

"Maybe," I said. I didn't truly *know* why, I thought. "Maybe," I said.

"Maybe it was just 'cause he was mean," Honey said. "Prob'ly Juliana is the goodest princess in the world."

Not like me, I thought. I shouldn't be mad at Dad. *He* wasn't mean, not really. He just felt bad, sometimes, and *acted* mean.

"He can't help himself, Gilly," Mar had told me. "He has such a temper, and he gets so depressed. Not being able to find a suitable job . . . It's hard on a man. It upsets him that he can't give us all the things he wants to. He loves us, Gilly. He really does. He just can't help himself . . ."

But still, I was feeling sore, a nagging, achy soreness in my chest, like a bruise. It was madness, and that was bad. It isn't his fault, I tried to tell myself, but still, it made me mad—him never letting me play with anyone.

"How did Juliana get out of the tower?" Honey wanted to know, but I couldn't think of an ending for the story.

"I'll tell you tomorrow night," I said.

I USED to have friends. When we lived in our other house, I had a friend named Leann. We went to the same babysitter and were in the same room at school. She sat at my table, and at lunchtime we ate together. After school, Leann and I walked to the babysitter's. Leann used to play pretend with me, and I remember she was good at coloring, but I could cut on the lines better than she could. I stayed overnight at her house once. And sometimes she came to my house to play. But that was before we moved. Before Mar finished college and went to work at the hospital. Before Dad started . . . before the secret.

WHENEVER I felt lonely, I liked to think about Juliana and her friends.

They play together in the kingdom of flowers, I liked to think. *They laugh and talk and share secrets. They play dress-up in the queen's cast-off gowns. They play with golden tops and balls and ride their ponies across the lawn, and when they get tired, clowns and jugglers make them laugh.*

Juliana is a princess, and princesses are special.
Princesses have friends.

I HAD SAID "OK" to Mary Rose when she asked me to walk to school with her. What would she think if I wasn't there the next morning, waiting on the corner? What would she think if I was? I thought about it that night as I waited for Dad to go to bed.

Listening for Dad kept me awake, and so did the ache in my chest . . .

I wondered why a girl like Mary Rose would *want* to walk to school with a girl like me. Maybe she didn't know about me. Maybe the other kids hadn't told her. Or maybe . . . maybe she didn't care. What if I just did go ahead and meet her tomorrow? She wouldn't have asked me if she hadn't wanted me to, I thought.

And Dad . . . Dad hadn't said I couldn't *walk to school* with Mary Rose. He had just said not to go "running off" to play with her . . .

I felt myself drift toward sleep, snuggled warm against Honey. Soft and golden, a picture of me and Mary Rose walking together down the street filled my head.

I came awake suddenly, just for a moment, and listened hard as Dad passed our door on the way to his and Mar's room. I heard their door close.

What if I did go meet Mary Rose on the corner, I thought, settling back into my pillow. I rubbed my cheek against the smooth, cool pillowcase. What if I did?

CHAPTER FOUR

HONEY WAS a sleepy-head when she first woke up. She made funny little grumbling noises and tried to burrow deeper under the covers. If I bounced on the bed, or played our game, "Borey-Borey-Bee," with her, sometimes I could start her laughing, and then she would wake up cheerfully and tumble out of bed to "get" me.

But the next morning, my head was too full of meeting-Mary-Rose-on-the-corner to take time to play games.

"C'mon, Honey, get up," I said, throwing her corduroy overalls at her. "C'mon, we'll be late."

"Mmm-frumf," Honey mumbled, curling herself into a ball.

"Honey!" I said. "Get up."

"Don' wanna," said Honey from under the covers.

I pulled her out, unwinding her from the warm blankets. She whimpered and shivered and tried to escape back to bed. I pulled off her nightie with one hand, keeping a tight hold on her goose-bumpy arm.

With her nightgown gone, Honey gave up and let me help her get dressed. But she insisted on tying her own shoelaces, which seemed to take forever. By the time we'd washed our faces and brushed our teeth, both of us were grumpy.

In the kitchen, Mar was standing by the stove in her blue bathrobe.

"Morning, chickens," she said, turning and giving us a sleepy-eyed smile. "How's French toast sound for breakfast?"

She put the spatula down and held out her arms and we kind of tumbled into her hug, Honey and me. Our grumps flew right out the door.

"How come you got up so early again?" I asked, snuggling against her.

"Oh, I get to missing my chicks. Haven't seen enough of you lately," Mar said.

My heart squeezed tight in my chest. Mar. Mar! I wished I could snuggle near her always and make her smile like this. I wished things were like they used to be!

What a rotten kid I was to even *think* of telling her about the secret, I told myself again. I mustn't worry her, I thought. I mustn't *ever* worry her. Besides, "Don't tell your mother," Dad had said.

MARY ROSE was waiting on the corner under her yellow umbrella when I came out our door. For a minute, feeling my heart begin to pound, I wanted to turn and run back in the house. But she grinned and waved at me. I took a deep breath and ran straight down the steps and into the mist before I had time to think.

"Hi," she yelled. "Hi, Gillian."

I ran across the street and skidded to a stop in front of her, gulping the cool, damp air.

"You're getting wet," she said and pulled me under her umbrella.

I couldn't think of a thing to say. I could feel her coat sleeve touching mine. My head bumped her umbrella, and I hunched my shoulders to make myself shorter, feeling embarrassed.

"We'll be late if we don't hurry," Mary Rose said and hooked her arm through mine.

It was not necessary, I found to my relief, to think of things to say to Mary Rose. She chatted away comfortably, leaving room only for my murmured "ums" and "ohs." Which was a good thing, because I could scarcely keep track of what she was saying, I was so giddy to be walking to school beside her.

I kept glancing at her face, lit golden by the yellow umbrella, and suddenly I knew why I had been drawn to watch her through the hedge.

I did not even think before the silly words came tumbling out. "Why, you are just like Juliana!" I said.

I HAD KNOWN how Juliana looked from the first time I made her up. When Juliana walked, I knew, she was so small and graceful, she seemed to dance. When she danced, she floated on air.

Juliana wasn't big for her age. *She* didn't stumble over cracks in the sidewalk or drop her books.

Juliana was fair. Her eyes were as blue as a summer sky. Her hair curled silken around her face.

No one made *her* wear bangs.

Juliana's gowns were especially for her—rose and scarlet and sunny gold, gossamer, silk and lace.

She didn't wear hand-me-downs.

THAT WAS why I said it. Mary Rose was just the way I wished I was—the way I imagined Juliana.

But I could have bitten off my tongue for saying so. What would Mary Rose think? I had ruined it already!

"Who's Juliana?" Mary Rose was asking as we stopped behind the safety patrol flag.

"Nobody," I muttered, my face hot.

"Is she someone in our class?"

I shook my head, longing for the traffic light to change. Tommy Hanson, the safety patrol guard, turned around and looked at me curiously.

"Well, who is she then?" Mary Rose insisted.

I heard the clicking of the traffic light control box on the telephone pole, and I saw the cars slowing. I ducked out from under Mary Rose's umbrella and brushed past Tommy's flag. I dashed across the street.

"Gillian?" I heard Mary Rose call after me.

And I heard Tommy telling her, "Gillian Harper's weird!"

HUDDLED in the farthest stall of the girls' rest room, I heard the first bell ring. The girls were laughing and talking as they turned off water or pulled down paper towels or flushed toilets and banged stall doors. Their voices sounded high and garbled, like a record played too fast. I thought they were probably talking about me, but my head ached so hard I couldn't make sense of their words.

The second bell rang. The voices faded. The last hurrying footsteps thudded down the hall, and the last door slammed.

Quiet.

It wrapped around me like a warm blanket. The only sound was the roaring ache in my head.

I stood up and leaned my forehead against the cool metal of the stall door. Little by little, the headache eased, and the sickness in my stomach unclutched. Finally, shakily, I was able to open the door and come out. I was shivering in my damp coat, but my face burned. I turned on the cold water and splashed some on my cheeks.

I was drying with a scratchy brown towel when the rest room door swung inward. Miss Gates poked her face through the crack.

"Gillian? Oh, good, you *are* in here. Michelle *said* she thought she'd seen you. Are you all right, dear?"

I nodded, feeling numb.

"Are you *sure* you feel all right, Gillian? You don't *look* well."

I glanced at myself in the mirror. My face stared back, the eyes too big, the mouth too pinched and white.

"I guess I don't feel very good," I said, and my voice came out a whisper.

Miss Gates came into the rest room and put her hand on my forehead. She looked at me thoughtfully. "Mary Rose said you ran away from her on the way to school today. She couldn't understand why. She was quite upset. Did you feel suddenly sick? Is that why you ran away?"

I shook my head, imagining the girls crowding around Miss Gates to talk about me. Please, I thought, please, Miss Gates, leave me alone.

"Mary Rose wasn't teasing you, was she, Gillian?"

"Oh no, Miss Gates." I was shocked at the idea. Mary Rose had been *nice* to me. It was *me* who had spoiled it. "No, Miss Gates. I . . . really don't feel good."

"Perhaps we had better send you home," Miss Gates said. "Is there someone at home who can come to get you, dear?"

My heart sank. Mar was probably asleep by now. But, undoubtedly, Dad was also at home. Dad would come to pick me up and take me home—alone—in the car with him.

"I don't feel *that* bad, Miss Gates," I said. "Really I don't. I'm OK now. I'm sorry. I'll come to class right away. I don't need to go home."

ALL DAY I could feel Mary Rose's eyes reproaching me. I didn't look at her. I kept my head down over my books. At lunchtime, I dawdled and got in line last so everyone in my class was seated by the time I got my lunch. Then I took my tray to the stage at one end of the cafeteria and sat on the steps. That was my favorite place to sit. I could read while I ate my lunch.

I couldn't help glancing, once, at Mary Rose. She was sitting with Michelle Shultz and Karen Davis and some of those kids. They were probably talking about me.

I SCOOTED out the door, grabbing my coat on the run, as soon as the last bell rang. I kept my eyes straight ahead and walked as fast as I could, taking the long way home. The rain had stopped. The sun was out, but it wasn't a warm sun, and I kept shivering as I walked, trying not to think how I had ruined everything.

It was just as well, I kept telling myself. Really, it was better. Better not to be friends with anyone. But deep inside me, someone was crying. Someone was feeling sad.

CHAPTER FIVE

HE NEXT DAY the sun shone again. When Honey and I went outdoors after school, we found the rhododendron blossoms had turned limp and brown around the edges. They hung forlornly from the spiky bunches of stamens or littered the ground beneath the bush.

"Where'd the pretty go?" Honey wailed when she saw them. "How can we make a Juliana doll?"

"Never mind about Juliana," I told her. "We'll think of another game, another story. Juliana was dumb anyway."

Honey pushed her lower lip out. "I *like* Juliana," she said.

But I was sick of Juliana. It was Juliana and all that dumb pretending that had gotten me into trouble with Mary Rose. "Go get one of your books, and I'll read to you," I told Honey.

But Honey just frowned and shook her head. "I want a made-up story," she said. "Not a book story. I want a Juliana story."

"Then you'll have to make it up yourself," I said. "I've got better things to do."

I left Honey standing next to the rhododendron bush

and wandered off across the yard. Better things to do. I
didn't really have better things to do. I didn't have anything to do at all until suppertime. I squatted down next
to the weed-grown flower bed that edged the foundation
of the house and tugged at some of the grass that had crept
out of the lawn and into the dirt of the bed. The grass
pulled loose from the dirt in a little mat. Where it had
been, the dirt looked dark and fresh and . . . somehow . . .
clean.

I could hear Honey snuffling over beside the rhododendron bush. I could also hear voices in the Gibbses' yard.
Painters were working on their house, scraping off the old,
flaky paint. A carpenter was building new steps to their
back door. His hammer made a sharp rat-a-tat-tat over the
hoarse scraping of the painters' tools.

Where I had pulled up the grass, two pale green leaves
were poking through the dirt. There had been flowers in
this bed last summer, I remembered. I could remember
yellow and red and orange and pink. They had been kind
of scraggly, choked and hidden among the weeds, but they
had been pretty and bright. I wondered if they would grow
better this year if I cleaned some of the weeds and grass
out of the bed the way the Gibbses had done in their yard.
It was pretty easy, now that I looked carefully, to see which
were the leaves of the new little flower plants and which
were dandelions and grass and other unwanted things.

I scooted to the end of the flower bed, next to the back
steps, so as to begin at the beginning, and started pulling

the weeds the way I had seen the Gibbses do. There were lots of weeds and not many little flower plants, but in just a few minutes I had cleared a clean, bare spot of earth. It looked nice, dark and glistening like fresh-cut chocolate cake. Most of the weeds pulled easily away from the rain-soaked dirt, roots and all, but a dandelion clung stubbornly, and only the leaves came away in my hand. I grubbed around the white, broken stub of the root with my fingers, but it broke again.

Honey clumped up the steps, still snuffling.

I knew she was giving me her accusing look, so I didn't glance up. I tried prying the dandelion root with a twig, but the twig broke, too.

Honey let the screen door slam.

I yanked at a clump of grass. I didn't have to entertain Honey every minute, I told myself, breathing hard through my nose. It felt good to tear out the grass and fling it on my growing pile of weeds.

I decided to leave the plants I wasn't absolutely certain were weeds. I began to make a game of getting the for-sure weeds up whole, trailing pale, dirt-crumbed traceries of root. I gave up on the dandelions after another try. Anyway, I decided I liked their yellow blossoms.

The knees of my jeans were soaked through as I crawled along the edge of the flower bed. My hands got muddy. Dirt caked under my nails.

The pile of weeds grew and grew. The moist, dark,

weeded flower bed stretched longer and longer as I scooted beside it. Here and there, the little plants I had left decorated it like frosting leaves.

At the corner of the house, I came to a clump of funny, bluish stems and spiky leaves. They were not any kind of flower I could think of. I tugged at them, thinking I'd clear them out, they looked so ugly flopped over in a blue-gray tangle; but they resisted me.

I sat back on my heels and surveyed what I had done. My nose was full of the clean, dark smell of damp earth, and I realized my breath came steady and calm. I decided to leave the strange, half-dead stems to wait and see if summer would revive them. The rest, I thought, was as good as Mary Rose could do. Better in fact, for I had noticed Mary Rose was impatient and slapdash in the way she worked.

And thinking of Mary Rose made me notice I couldn't hear voices from her yard any more. The tap-tap-tap was silent. There was no scraping sound. I saw it was getting late. The light had paled and shadowed. I shivered and realized I was cold.

I wiped my hands on my jeans and gathered up my armful of weeds. I carried them to the rubbish heap behind the walnut tree where Dad had thrown the old screen door and a punctured tire from the car.

I began to wonder what Honey was doing that had kept her quiet so long, and suddenly I felt uneasy. I should have checked on her, I thought. She could have gotten into something. She could have hurt herself.

My feet started hurrying toward the house.

She could have fallen and bumped her head. She could have turned on the stove. It would be my fault, I thought. I was breathing in gasps again.

"Honey," I called, scrambling up the back steps.

My fault.

"Honey!" I yelled, yanking open the door.

My fault.

It was Mr. Rogers's soothing voice that stopped me halfway across the kitchen. The TV was on.

I pressed my hand to my heart to slow it down.

Honey was watching TV, I thought. That's OK. She's just watching TV.

And then I saw Dad's jacket slung over the back of a chair.

I hadn't heard the car. I hadn't heard Dad calling me the way he usually did as he came in the house. But then, I hadn't heard the workmen leave the Gibbses' yard either. I hadn't noticed the daylight fade.

A beer bottle cap lay on the counter I had cleared before we went out to play.

Dad's home, I thought, home watching TV with Honey.

With a lurch, my heart began to pound again.

Standing in the unlighted kitchen, staring at the gleam of the beer bottle cap and listening to Mr. Rogers's pleasant, unhurried voice, I remembered how the secret had started last spring, watching TV with Dad.

IT WAS right after Mar started to work.

I had gotten up for a drink of water that first time. As I came down the hall from the bathroom, I could see the bluish eye of the TV shining into the hall from the living room. Dad was sitting in his big chair. I could see the top of his curly head.

It was something about a circus on the TV. I could hear the circus music, kind of tinkly, and see a lady in a spangly purple outfit getting ready to swing on a trapeze. I thought I'd just watch for a minute—to see the lady do her tricks.

The lady flew through the air straight to the hands of a man who was hanging by his knees. She turned somer-saults in the air and did flip-flops that made me catch my breath. I edged into the living room to watch. After the trapeze lady, it was clowns. I had to put my hand over my mouth to keep from laughing out loud. And then the commercial came on.

"Gilly."

I jumped when Dad spoke to me.

"Come here," Dad said, but his voice didn't sound mad. "What are you doing up so late, young lady?" He lifted me into his lap.

I was so relieved. He *wasn't* mad. "I just wanted a drink of water," I said.

I remember him laughing. "No water in the living room," he said. But he didn't tell me to go back to bed. He just pulled me closer and nuzzled me on my neck.

The program came on again. Now it was some kids doing tricks on the backs of little ponies.

Dad rubbed my chest. His hand felt big and warm. He rubbed my tummy under my nightgown. His mouth was wet when he kissed me, and I wondered why.

Suddenly my stomach felt funny. It was different—the way he was touching me. It didn't feel good.

"It's all right, Baby," Dad said, his voice sounding quick and choky.

But I said, "I've got to go to the bathroom, Dad," and I wriggled off his lap, pulling away from the scary touch. I ran back down the hall. There was a red mark on my arm where he tried to hang on to me. Later it turned into a bruise.

NOW *Honey* was alone with Dad, watching TV. I made myself move. I made myself put one foot in front of the other, slowly, my knees shaking as I walked across the kitchen.

It was dark in the hall. I felt my way along the wall toward the light of the living room doorway. It was the light of the television, the flickering bluish light.

There was such a loud noise in my head I thought Dad would hear me. It was hard to make myself look into the living room, hard to make myself look for Dad's dark, curly head above the back of his chair. But I did. I lifted my eyes and peered through the dimness and saw he was there, in his chair in front of the TV.

Deep inside me, someone was beginning to cry. But *I* was not making a sound. I was moving around Dad's chair, anger rising strong and loud inside me with the loudness in my head.

Honey was sitting on Dad's lap.

I let out a cry, half-strangled, that grated, hurting in my throat, and lunged at them.

Dad's head, which had been leaning against the back of his chair, came up, and his eyes popped open, surprised.

I saw that his hands were resting on the arms of the chair. I saw that Honey was sitting, playing with some pop beads, on his knees. I saw she was wearing her overalls, and they were buttoned up.

"Chrissake!" barked Dad. "What are you doing? You startled me!"

I had checked in mid-lunge and turned and fallen against his leg all in one motion.

"Nothing," I said, flopping over onto my stomach and pretending to watch the screen. I could feel the crying beginning, and I struggled to keep it back.

Honey scrambled off Dad's knees and jumped on me, clutching me around my neck. "You start'ed me, Gilly!" she yelled. "You start'ed me!"

I rolled over, away from Dad's leg, and pulled her into a hug, burying my face against her overalls bib. I wiped my wet cheeks against the corduroy and hugged her hard.

Not Honey. Not Honey.

Only me.

CHAPTER SIX

THE NEXT WEEK, Mary Rose stopped coming to class. One day. Two days. Three days. Mary Rose's seat was empty. I didn't have to avoid her on the way to school.

On Friday, Miss Gates called me to her desk just before the last bell rang.

"Mary Rose has hurt her ankle," Miss Gates said. "Mrs. Gibbs called and asked if someone could bring Mary Rose's books to her. It may be a while before she can return to school."

I didn't know what to say.

"I believe you live near Mary Rose, don't you, Gillian?" Miss Gates said. "Would you please gather her books and folders out of her desk and take them and this list of assignments to her?"

"Couldn't someone else do it, Miss Gates?" I said.

"Why, Gillian . . . is it inconvenient for you?" Miss Gates said. "Is there some reason you can't?"

"N-n-no," I said, looking at the floor. I couldn't think of a reason. "No."

"I would very much appreciate it if you would, Gillian," Miss Gates said. "I'm sure Mary Rose will appreciate it, too."

She handed me the list of assignments, neatly written out in her firm, round handwriting. The bell rang. People started talking, and someone flung open the door to the hall. Some of the boys had sprinted out of the room before I could take the list from Miss Gates's hand.

"Thank you, Gillian," Miss Gates said, raising her voice over the commotion. She was smiling at me. Encouragingly, I thought.

I went to my desk and got out my library book. As usual, I had already finished my homework. Then I went to Mary Rose's desk and opened the top.

Mary Rose's books and papers were all a-clutter. Loose papers were crumpled in among the scrunched and folded pages of her books. There were pencils and a ruler and two pairs of scissors. A giant crayon box with its top torn off spilled worn and broken crayons.

I sighed and set about smoothing papers and closing and stacking books. Mary Rose's desk looked, I thought, like Honey's half of our room. "Lived in," Mar called it, laughingly.

The classroom had emptied. Miss Gates was getting her purse out of her bottom drawer.

"Thank you again, Gillian," she said, and then she was gone, too.

As long as I was at it, I thought I'd just as well clean up the mess. I poked the crayons back into the box, trying to match up broken halves. I gathered the pencils and put them together at the front of the desk. Then I began to sort the papers. Lots of them had been crumpled up, ready to thrown away. Obviously, Mary Rose just hadn't gotten them to the wastebasket. But a few looked like they might be important. I piled the throwaway papers on her seat and smoothed out the rest to put into her folder—a half-finished math assignment, an unfinished test and what looked like a letter.

My hand stopped suddenly as I reached into the desk for a torn tablet sheet. My eye had been caught by my own name.

Gillian.

It was Mary Rose's helter-skelter handwriting.

She had drawn a scribble of circles around my name and some arrows pointing to it and three big question marks. Then she had started to write my whole name, Gillian Harper. Only that was where the paper was torn, so it read, Gillian Har . . .

My hand moved slowly to pick the paper up. I turned it over. There was nothing on the other side. Then I saw another torn piece, poking out from beneath a social studies book. I pulled it out and fitted it to the piece in my hand. They matched.

I stared at the paper in astonishment. It was several seconds before I realized my mouth was gaping. I closed it and swallowed hard.

Me? Pretty? Everybody knew I got good grades, but

Gillian

? ? ?

Gillian Harper

Pretty

Smart

Mysterious !!!

I wonder why she doesn't like me?
Is it because I talk too much?
? ? ? ? ? ? ? ? ? ? ? ? ? ? ? ?

pretty? Me? And mysterious? (Mary Rose had misspelled it, but I knew what she meant.) Mysterious! That was what the other kids called weird!

Mary Rose thought *I* didn't like *her*!

High heels clicked outside the classroom door. I dropped the torn pieces into the desk and bent over hurriedly to gather the papers I had put on Mary Rose's seat. When Miss Gates came back into the room, I had my back to her, my face hidden, scurrying toward the wastebasket, to throw them away.

"You still here, Gillian? My goodness, you don't have to clean up Mary Rose's desk," Miss Gates said. She clicked toward the desk, and I dumped the crumpled papers and whirled, realizing she was going to look into it and see the torn paper.

"I just thought . . ." I said, my voice sounding breathless and shrill.

But Miss Gates only glanced at what I had done and smiled. "How very thoughtful of you, Gillian. Mary Rose could learn a lesson in neatness from you."

"That's OK," I said, hurrying back and gathering up Mary Rose's books. "I don't mind. Good-bye, Miss Gates."

"Good-bye, Gillian. Have a nice weekend." She sat down at her desk, took up a notepad and examined something written there.

" 'Bye," I said as I put the top down on Mary Rose's desk and scooted for the coat closet. The torn paper was tucked safely inside Mary Rose's folder where I had slipped it as I gathered up the books.

In the hall, I had to stop to catch my breath. I took the torn paper out of the folder, folded the two pieces together and put them in my coat pocket. I didn't dare look at them. My heart was thumping, and there was a tickly feeling in my stomach.

Gillian Harper—pretty, I thought, and the thought bubbled so happily in my brain it made me feel scared.

She thought *I* didn't like *her*!

I didn't have time to take Mary Rose's books to her before I went home. I was late. Honey would be home from preschool soon.

I ran all the way.

THE FRONT DOOR was unlocked, and the TV was on.

"Honey?" I called as I pushed open the door. "Honey, I'm home."

"Hi, Gil," Dad said from the couch.

I closed the door behind me and clutched Mary Rose's books to my chest.

"Hi, Dad," I said. "I'm sorry I'm late. Where's Honey?"

Dad was stretched out on the couch in his bathrobe. He had a can of beer in his hand, and more cans littered the carpet around him. The drapes shut out the afternoon sun.

"Did you have a nice day at school?" Dad asked.

His chin was smudgy with unshaved beard.

I nodded and measured the distance to the hall door with my eyes. I began to edge toward it.

"Where's Honey?" I asked.

"Won't be home until later. One of her little pals is having a birthday party." He smiled, and the smile made my neck feel crawly. "So you and I can have a nice time," he said.

"I've got to run over to the neighbors' for a minute, Dad," I said, my voice hurrying as my feet began to move across the room. "Got to take some books to a girl from school."

"Gilly!" His voice stopped me before I reached the door.

"Please, Dad," I said. "I told Miss Gates I'd take them to her."

"You can do it later."

"But, Dad . . ."

"Put the books down and take off your coat and come here, Gilly!"

When he saw me put the books on a chair, his voice got soft. "Come on, Baby. Come on. Come to Dad."

"Please, Dad," I said again, hopelessly. "Please."

"Come keep Dad company, Baby," Dad said. "Come on now. I've been waiting for you to get home. I've been waiting and thinking about you."

I dragged across the living room, pulled by my dad's voice like a puppy on a leash. Dad wasn't looking at my face, and I didn't want to look at his. I watched the TV. "Please, Dad," I said again, but his hand reached out and grabbed me and jerked me to the couch.

He took a long drink from his can of beer and then dropped it, empty, to the carpet. He lifted me onto the couch beside him and pulled up my dress.

I tried to pull away. The smothery feeling was coming fast, so I kept my eyes on the TV screen, where some cowboys were shooting guns. Dad held my arms tight, so I couldn't move.

"It's all right, Baby," Dad said. He was breathing hard. "Ah," he said. "Ah, Baby."

My head was getting dizzy, and a beery smell was in my nose, and a bad taste came in my mouth when he put his hand over it.

Inside me, someone had begun to scream. "Stop, stop, stop," she screamed. It was Juliana.

Poor Juliana. The beast had gotten her again. The beast with the bloody eyes and the drooling mouth and the breath that smelled of death. The beast had pounced on Juliana and was devouring her.

Poor Juliana. She screamed and screamed. I tried to tell her not to worry. I tried to tell her not to be afraid. The king will come soon to rescue you, I told her. You will be saved.

But the beast kept devouring Juliana, and she kept on screaming for a long, long time.

CHAPTER SEVEN

 I DIDN'T TAKE Mary Rose's books to her that afternoon.

"I'm sorry, Baby," Dad said afterwards, like he always did. "You're getting to be so sexy, I just can't help myself."

So it *had* to be my fault.

I had tried to blame it on other things—on moving last spring, on Mar 'cause she went to work. But it wasn't that. It was me.

"You're getting so sexy," Dad said. Dad hugged me and patted my back.

I couldn't help crying.

"I didn't hurt you, Gilly," said Dad, and now his voice was sounding scared. "Stop crying. You know you really like it."

I *don't* like it, I cried inside myself. I don't. I don't. But deep, deep down, I knew that sometimes, for a minute, I did. Sometimes, for a little while, it felt good.

It *was* me who had started changing. I could see it in the mirror when I took my bath. I could feel it with my hands.

"Growing up," Mar said.

That was why I knew it really *was* my fault. I don't *want* to grow up, I thought, and cried harder.

"That's enough, young lady," Dad said now. "Stop crying." He pushed me away.

"I can't help it," I said. I rubbed my arm across my eyes and tried to stand up. My legs felt weak.

"Chrissakes!" Dad yelled. "You're not hurt. If you're going to carry on like this, I won't ever touch you again."

For a moment, I felt a flicker of hope. It died.

He had said that before. "I'm sorry. It won't happen again," he had said. But it always did. Sooner or later.

Sooner or later, "Come keep me company," Dad would say.

MARY ROSE'S BOOKS sat where I had left them on the living room chair. When I went into the living room next morning, they were there, waiting for me. Waiting for me to take them to Mary Rose.

I just couldn't. I had been stupid to think I could ever face Mary Rose again.

I took the torn tablet page out of my pocket. I didn't look at it. I folded it into smaller and smaller squares and tucked it inside my fairy tale book.

When Mar got up late that Saturday morning, she said we were going to clean house.

"This place is a mess," Mar said. "I need help cleaning it up. I can't do everything! Not work fulltime *and* take care of the house and you girls by myself."

You don't take care of us, I thought. I take care of Honey, and nobody takes care of *me*!

But I didn't say anything. Mar was talking to Dad anyway, not to me. I could tell by the way she watched him, from the corner of her eye.

He didn't say anything either, or even move, except to turn the pages of his paper.

Mar pushed back her chair with an abrupt, scraping noise and began to stack dishes to carry them to the sink. The dishes made an angry clatter.

"Clear the table, girls," Mar said.

Honey climbed out of her booster chair, and I handed her my glass to carry to Mar. I picked up the butter dish and the orange juice jug and took them to the frig.

Crash!

I whirled to see Honey, her eyes squinched shut and her face turning red, opening her mouth to howl. The glass was in a million pieces on the floor.

"Did you give her that glass?" Mar yelled at me. "You know better than that!"

Honey bellowed.

Mar snatched her out of the broken glass and plunked her on a chair. "I can't turn my back for one minute," Mar yelled. "You don't give a five-year-old a slippery glass, Gilly! What were you thinking of?"

Honey howled.

Dad pushed back his chair and slapped the paper on the edge of the table. "Chrissakes!" he said. "A man can't read in peace around here! I'm going out."

"Where?" Mar said, reaching for the broom. "Where are you going?"

But Dad didn't answer. He just stomped out of the kitchen, and a minute later, the front door slammed.

Mar jabbed at the broken glass with the broom. Honey was snuffling and rubbing her fists in her eyes.

"Hold the dustpan, at least," Mar told me, and I slammed the refrigerator door and ran to do what she said.

When I knelt, holding the dustpan, I saw there were tears in Mar's eyes. "I can't do it all myself," I heard her mutter as the broom flicked the shards of glass into the pan.

"I'm sorry, Mar," I said. "I'm sorry. What should I do to help?"

"PUT THESE in your room where they belong," Mar said, handing me the stack of Mary Rose's books. We had finished the kitchen and bathroom and were cleaning the living room, Mar and me. Honey was taking a nap.

"They're not mine," I said.

"Whose are they then?"

"Mary Rose Gibbs's. She got a broken foot or something, and Miss Gates asked me to take them to her."

"Mary Rose . . . ? Oh, one of those new girls?" Mar pushed back her hair. "The ones behind us?" she said.

I nodded.

"Well, then, why didn't you? Why are they sitting here in our living room?"

I looked at the carpet, tracing the swirls of green and brown with my eyes. I could feel my face getting hot.

"That's not very responsible, Gilly," Mar said sternly. "You should have taken them straight over after school."

"I know," I said, hanging my head.

"Oh, Gilly!" Mar said. She put her hands on my shoulders. "What in the world is wrong with you? I've never seen such a kid for moping. I swear, I could hang a coat on your lower lip, it's pushed out so far!"

I looked up at her through my eyelashes and saw her head shake back and forth, softly, softly. There was a little sad smile in her eyes.

I had to smile back. The vision of a coat hanging from my lower lip was pretty silly!

"We've just about finished here," Mar said and gave me a hug. "Why don't you scoot over now and take Mary What's-her-name's books to her?"

I couldn't hug her back 'cause my arms were full of books, but, "OK," I said. "OK."

She let me go and gave me a little pat.

I was in the doorway when she spoke again. "Gilly," she said. "Why don't you stay and visit with Mary for a while? She might be lonely."

"OK," I said. I went to the closet to get my jacket.

"And Gilly . . ." Mar said, poking her head out the

living room doorway. "Thank you for helping. I'm sorry I was cross. You really *are* a very big help."

I THOUGHT I'd go through the hedge to Mary Rose's house. But once I was in the back yard, carried *that* far on Mar's smile, I found I just couldn't do it.

I didn't know whether to go to the back door or the front. I didn't know whether to knock or ring the bell. And what if no one came to the door? And what if someone did? What would I say? And what would I do? And how would I explain why I hadn't brought the books yesterday?

I stood beside the rhododendron bush, the books in my arms, and I couldn't go any farther. But I couldn't go back either. Mar thought I was visiting Mary Rose.

I knelt, and shoving the books before me, I crawled under the rhododendron bush. I put the books on my jacket to keep them dry, and then I settled my back against the trunk and hugged my arms around my knees. I closed my eyes and let the stillness fold around me.

In the hedge, a bird was rustling. Next door, the neighbor's dog made gentle, snuffling sounds. I breathed the clean, safe smell of earth and felt its solid damp.

The wonderful thing about Juliana, I thought, was Juliana was enchanted. What that meant was she couldn't be hurt. Not really hurt. When bad things happen to princesses, someone always rescues them. The dragons are slain, the towers are unlocked. When a beast ate up Juliana, it only *seemed* that way. Next morning, she would awaken, whole and new. If she fell into a bog, a magic spring would wash her clean. If she went to sleep a hundred years, a kiss would break the spell. The wonderful thing about Juliana was she was enchanted. *Her* bad things weren't real.

CHAPTER EIGHT

THE GIBBSES' back door banged.

I knelt forward and peered through the hedge.

"Be back in a sec," Daphne Gibbs called over her shoulder. She was poised at the top of their new, unpainted steps. She ran down the steps, bounded across the yard, and before I could realize what was happening, she poked her head into the hedge and looked straight into my eyes.

"Oh," Daphne said, her gray eyes opening wide to match her O-shaped mouth. "Oh dear! I didn't know someone was here!"

I stared at her.

Daphne giggled. "I was looking for a way through the hedge," she said.

I pointed.

"Thanks," said Daphne. "Is it OK if I come through?"

I nodded, and in a moment she was on our side.

"Where are you?" Daphne said, brushing a spiderweb off her nose.

I crawled out of the rhododendron bush.

"Hey," said Daphne. "What a neat hiding place! I used to have a place like that at our old house—under the porch."

I nodded, my mind blank. I couldn't think what to say.

"I'm Daphne Gibbs," Daphne said. "Are you Gillian Harper? Mose *said* you were the quiet type."

"Mose?" I said.

She smiled. "It's what I call her—my sister, Mary Rose. Isn't that a dumb name? Mary Rose? We both have dumb names. Flower names—Rose and Daphne. It's 'cause our mom is crazy about flowers."

"Flowers?" I said. "Daphne?"

"Yeah, Daphne's a flower. We just planted a daphne bush in our front yard. I'll show you sometime."

"Oh," I said, feeling strangely pleased. "*I* think your name is beautiful!" I didn't say, just like you, but I was thinking it. Where Mary Rose's eyes were sparkly blue, Daphne's were a soft, clear gray. Where Mary Rose's hair was shiny gold, Daphne's hair was honey. Daphne was thinner, paler, more grown-up. "Beautiful!" I said.

"Dumb!" laughed Daphne. "Mose calls me 'Daffy.' You can too, if you want."

"They call me 'Gilly,' " I said.

"Gilly?" Daphne sounded surprised. "Why then, *you* have a flower name, too!"

"I do?" I said.

"Sure. Gillyflower. It's kind of like a carnation, only littler. Some people call them 'pinks,' I think. They smell real nice, kind of spicy-sweet."

"They *do*?" I said.

"Yeah," she said. "Well, join the club, Gilly. We've all got dumb flower names."

Daphne had come over to get Mary Rose's books.

"Miss Gates told Mom she'd give them to you," she said.

I felt myself blushing. "I . . . I meant to bring them over yesterday . . ." I stammered.

"That's OK," Daphne said. "Mose's ankle was really hurting yesterday. She didn't do anything but sleep and groan. She wouldn't have used them. But she's better today."

"Just a minute," I said, and I crawled halfway into the rhododendron bush and pulled out the stack of books. I thought Daphne looked at me funny as I handed them to her, but she didn't say anything, so I didn't have to explain what Mary Rose's books were doing in the bush.

"Thanks," Daphne said. "Want to come over and see her?"

"Uh . . ." I said. "Uh, no, I better not."

"C'mon," said Daphne. "I know she'd love it. She gets really bored just lying there!"

"Uh . . ." I said, but Daphne wasn't listening to me. She grabbed my hand and pulled me through the hedge.

Mary Rose's house smelled of new paint. Mrs. Gibbs was sitting at a sewing machine set up by the dining room window.

"Running up a hem on the kitchen curtains," she explained when Daphne introduced me. "Excuse me for not getting up. Just go right on in. Daphne, show Gilly where. Mary Rose will be thrilled to see you, Gilly. She's an impossible patient—I might almost say an impossible 'impatient'!"

I smiled. It sounded like one of Mar's jokes.

"Right in there," Daphne said, as she opened the door at the end of the hall.

If Daphne hadn't been standing there, looking at me expectantly, I don't suppose I'd have had the nerve to walk through that door. But Daphne *was* standing there, and so I did.

Mary Rose was sitting up in bed, her hurt leg propped on pillows. A family of paper dolls and their clothes were spread over her blanketed knees. "Gillian!" she said. "Hi!"

I didn't know what to say, or where to look, and so I found myself staring at the paper dolls.

Mary Rose's hands began to move nervously, gathering up the dolls and stuffing them into an old stationery box. "I don't usually play with these dumb things," she said. "I was just so *bored*."

I raised my eyes to her face and was astonished to see how pink it was. Mary Rose was blushing!

"I like to play paper dolls," I found myself saying, softly.

"You do?" Mary Rose's hands hovered over the box. The dolls were getting bent and crumpled, she had shoved them in so hastily.

"Mmm-hmm," I murmured, and without thinking

what I was doing, I moved to the side of the bed and began to smooth out the paper clothes and rearrange them in the box.

Mary Rose patted the bed beside her. "Sit here," she said, and so I did. Mary Rose put her hand on my arm, and I stopped tidying the dolls and looked at her. She was smiling, and the blush was gone. "I do too," she said. "Really I do. I just thought *you'd* think paper dolls were baby stuff."

"I don't," I said, caught by the warmth in her eyes.

"Then, why don't we play together?" Mary Rose said.

And so we did.

"WHERE HAVE *you* been?" Dad asked.

"I . . . uh . . ."

"She's been playing at the neighbors'," Mar told him. "I said she could."

"With those high and mighty types behind us?" Dad said. "I wouldn't think *our* kid would be good enough for *their* little darlings."

Mar wiped her hands on a towel and tossed it on the counter. "Don't be silly, Sid," she said, and her voice sounded tired. "You don't even *know* the people."

Dad pushed away from the refrigerator, where he had been leaning, watching Mar peel potatoes at the sink. He yanked open the refrigerator door and got out a beer. "I can see what they're doing to their house, can't I?" he said, jerking the tab and gulping a big mouthful. "First thing you know, property values'll go up, and *we* won't be able to afford the rent!"

I saw Mar sigh and press her lips together as she filled a pan with water. I edged toward the door, hoping Dad had forgotten me. On my way, I picked up the towel from the counter, folded it and hung it up.

"I thought you said this morning you needed help with the housework," Dad said. "Didn't you need *her* help?"

I stopped in my tracks, scarcely breathing. I kept my head down, my eyes on the floor. Don't fight about *me*, I prayed.

"She *did* help," Mar said, "unlike some I could name. She was a big help."

"I'll bet!" Dad said.

Mar pressed her lips together tight again. She was dropping the peeled potatoes into the pan on the stove.

"I don't like it," Dad said. "I don't like it a bit!"

"What's the big deal, Sid? She just went to play with a neighbor kid on a Saturday afternoon. She's entitled. She's just a kid herself!"

Dad glared. He rubbed the cold beer can against his cheek.

I took another quiet step toward the door.

"Hey," said Dad, and glancing up, I saw his eyes narrow. "Hey, isn't that the kid I told you not to play with?"

"You said not after school," I muttered and desperately took another step.

"I thought so! I thought it was. I told her not to play with that kid," he said to Mar, triumphantly.

"For heaven's sake, why not?" Mar said.

"Because *I* said so, that's why!" Dad banged the can down on the kitchen counter, and I jumped. Some beer foamed out of the hole in the top. "Those people are Class A snobs, and I don't want my kid over there. Period."

Mar turned away from the stove and put her hands on her hips. She stared at Dad. "There is *nothing* wrong with those people, Sid," she said, her voice tight and quiet. "They are just fixing up their own house, which they have a perfect right to do. We'd do it ourselves if we had the money."

Dad stared back at her for a moment, and then his shoulders slumped. "That again," he said. "Always that. It's too bad you married such a failure, Pat." He spun and stomped out of the kitchen.

"Oh, Sid," Mar said, with a kind of helplessness in her voice. "Oh, Sid."

CHAPTER NINE

 OME SEE ME AGAIN," Mary Rose had said. "Promise?"

And I had said, "I promise."

I wanted to keep my promise. But I was scared. Dad would be angry if he found out I went to play with her again. It might cause trouble for Mar. I had a shaky feeling in my stomach when I thought about it. But then I would think about the way Mary Rose and I had played paper dolls, and the shaky feeling would change to a tickle—a tiny tickle of happiness. Mary Rose liked me! "Come see me again," she had said, and her voice had sounded as if she meant it, as if she *really* wanted me to come.

I suppose that's why, on Monday after school, I found myself standing by the hedge with Honey, looking into the Gibbses' yard.

Dad wasn't home, and I didn't know when he'd be home. I won't stay long, I told myself. He'll never even know we've been gone.

"It's a secret," I told Honey. "Don't tell anyone."

"Like my secret?" Honey asked, and my heart stood still.

"What secret?" I said, my voice sounding choky.

"It's a secret!" Honey said. "You can't trick me, Gilly. I can keep a secret."

I looked hard at her funny, laughing face, at her crinkled-at-the-corners eyes, and—it can't be *that*, I thought. I'm imagining things. Not Honey. She's too little. It can't be a secret with Dad!

"You're pretty smart, Honeybee," I said and took her sticky little hand in mine and helped her through the hedge.

"I *had* to bring her," I told Mary Rose, feeling anxious. "I have to take care of her after school."

But Mary Rose didn't seem to mind, and she did seem really glad to see us. "You're lucky to have a *little* sister, Gilly," she said. "Big ones are *such* a pain!"

Daphne yelped and threw a slipper at her, and Honey, delighted, dived to retrieve it and throw it back. Her aim was bad, and the slipper skittered under the bed. While we were all laughing, and Mary Rose was hanging over the side of the bed trying to see where it had gone, Mrs. Gibbs came into the bedroom with some cookies and juice on a tray.

"Calm down, girls," she said. "Doctor says Mary Rose must keep quiet, or she can't go back to school next week."

Mary Rose righted herself and leaned back against her pillow. "It's so *boring!*" she said. "Just lying here. There's nothing to do!"

"There's schoolwork to do," Mrs. Gibbs said, sounding just like Mar.

"Nothing *fun* to do," Mary Rose said.

Mrs. Gibbs clucked her tongue and shook her head as she left the room.

"Fun or not, I guess I'd better get at my homework," Daphne said, reaching for a handful of cookies and a glass of juice, and then she left, too.

Honey was sidling over to the nightstand, where Mrs. Gibbs had set the tray. Her eyes were fixed on the plate of cookies, though she held her hands behind her back.

"Would you like a cookie, Beatrice?" Mary Rose said.

Honey's face lighted, and her hand reached out eagerly.

"Sit down on the floor," I ordered, intercepting the grabbing hand. I chose a plastic cup from the tray.

Honey sat down obediently, and I handed her the cup and fixed a couple of cookies on a napkin in front of her.

"Don't spill," I said.

"It *is* boring," Mary Rose said, offering me the cookie plate. "Take my advice. Don't ever tear ligaments in your ankle. It hurts, and worst of all, it's boring, boring, boring!"

"OK," I said, nibbling at a cookie. With Daphne and Mrs. Gibbs gone, and Honey busy with her cookies and juice, I felt awkward, standing there beside the bed, looking at Mary Rose. "Want to play paper dolls?" I said to fill the silence that was suddenly between us.

"I'm *tired* of paper dolls," said Mary Rose.

"Oh." And then there was silence again.

"Do you have any games?" I said desperately.

"Yeah, but I'm tired of them, too."

"Well, what *do* you want to do?"

"I don't know. What do *you* want to do?"

"I don't know," I said.

"Tell us a story, Gilly," Honey said. "Tell us a Juliana story."

"Juliana?" Mary Rose said. "Hey, who is this Juliana anyway?"

So that's how I came to tell Mary Rose about Juliana. Not everything, of course. Not about actually pretending *I* was Juliana. Not about feeling Juliana all mixed up inside me. Certainly not about Dad. But I found myself telling her the rest. About how I had made Juliana up, about the dolls made of rhododendron blossoms, about princesses and kingdoms and dancing and stuff.

Honey had climbed up on the bed. "I *love* Juliana," she said. "Tell about Juliana and the tower, Gilly. Tell about the beast."

"But you said—that day walking to school—you said *I* was like Juliana," Mary Rose said.

"Well," I said, drawing circles around the dots on her bedspread with my fingertip, "well, just that you're so pretty and all."

"Me?" said Mary Rose, and I could see she wasn't laughing at me. "Me?" she said. "But I'm runty and washed-out pale. *I've* always wanted to look like *you*: tall and dark and filled out. I don't s'pose I'll *ever* develop. I'm probably going to be a stringbean all my life!"

I looked at her in astonishment. "Why, Mary Rose," I said. "Why, Mary Rose!"

WE HAD STAYED too long at Mary Rose's house. As we slipped back through the hedge, I could see someone had turned on the lights in the kitchen.

"Dad's home," I told Honey, my heart jerking in my chest. "I'd better tell him where we were. He'll find out anyway. I'll tell him it's my fault."

I don't care, my heart was saying as it beat. I don't care! It had been worth it, to spend the afternoon with Mary Rose. It had been worth anything!

But when I shoved open the kitchen door, Dad didn't even turn around from where he was standing, stirring something on the stove.

"Hi, Dad," I said. "We were just . . ."

"Go wash your hands," Dad said. "I've got some spaghetti heating. Go wash your hands and then get the table set."

For a minute, I couldn't believe it. He wasn't going to ask where we'd been. He wasn't even going to be mad that we weren't home!

"Yes, sir," I said, shoving Honey ahead of me toward the bathroom. "Yes, sir!"

THAT WAS the beginning of a happy time.

Mary Rose said I was her best friend. I sneaked over

to her house almost every day. And the next week, when she started back to school, I carried her books for her because she couldn't manage them and her crutches too. And I got her tray for her at lunchtime, and she wanted to sit with *me*. And after school, Mrs. Gibbs gave me a ride when she came to drive Mary Rose home.

One day, I went to the library and checked out ten books, five on my card and five on Mary Rose's.

"Oh, they all look so good, I don't know which I want to read," Mary Rose said. "When I've finished mine, let's trade."

So that was what we did, and kept on doing every week. After a while, Mary Rose's ankle was well enough so we could walk to the library together. She liked all the books I liked—*Baby Island* and *Boxcar Children* and *Where the Wild Fern Grows*.

She liked the same games too—paper dolls and dress-up and coloring and pretend—games the other girls thought were baby stuff.

And Mary Rose *didn't* like PE, just like me, and she was bad at math, too.

Mary Rose said that being best friends meant we had to tell each other our secrets. She told me about Daphne's boyfriend, and she admitted that she, Mary Rose, thought boys were *kind of* interesting, but we both vowed we'd never be silly over boys the way Daphne was. Mary Rose said she was afraid she would get a C in math. She told me how she hid the ugly sweater her aunt gave her for Christmas and told her mother it was lost. And I told Mary Rose *my* secrets. Well, I told her *most* of them.

Sometimes, I told Juliana stories to Mary Rose and Honey. Sometimes we played pretend. We made dancing gowns out of Mrs. Gibbs's old scarves. Barefooted, we danced Juliana dances, Mary Rose and me. I climbed into the walnut tree, and I was Juliana, locked in the tower, and Mary Rose rescued me. Mary Rose hid in the closet, and she was Juliana, hiding from the beast. Honey liked to snuffle through her nose and growl, looking more like a kitten than a terrible beast, and Mary Rose would shriek in terror, and I would rescue her.

CHAPTER TEN

HE GIBBSES' GARDEN GREW, and so did my flowers. They got bigger and greener, and round, bright leaves unfolded on graceful, curling stems.

I kept the flower bed weeded—the weeds grew faster than the flowers—and Mary Rose showed me how to get dandelions out with a weeding fork her mother lent us. Mary Rose also showed me the rosebush her family had planted that was her very own. "Our Mary-Rose bush," Mrs. Gibbs called it. And the daphne that was Daphne's.

"Daphne blooms in early spring, but we'll have to wait until summer for *my* flowers," Mary Rose said.

"We ought to plant some gillyflowers for Gilly," Daphne said, and I blushed and felt pleased, but, of course, they never got around to it. The Gibbses were busy that spring, working in their yard and fixing up their house.

The days passed, some wet, some bright, and I sneaked over to Mary Rose's whenever I got a chance, and I worked in my flower bed. "Come go to the store with me, Gilly," Dad said sometimes, or, "You can stay up late with me tonight," or "Keep me company." But when it happened, I closed my eyes tight, and Juliana came. When Dad looked at me funny, I thought of Juliana dancing. When he came into the bathroom and wanted to help me wash, I thought of Juliana and the magic spring. I stayed away from him when he was watching TV, and I tried to go to bed when Honey did. But often that spring, he wasn't there when I got home from school; and more and more, he didn't stay home after we went to bed.

"You take care of things, Gilly," he would tell me when he went out.

"I will, Dad," I told him. "I will," and I liked the long, comfortable evenings when Dad wasn't home.

One night, Mar got home before Dad did. I heard the yelling when he came in. I heard the doors slamming and the roar of the car when Dad took off again. I heard Mar cry.

I got up and crept to Mar's bedroom, feeling scared. Mar's eyes were weepy-red, and she hugged me so hard it almost hurt.

"Don't worry, chicken," she said. "It'll be OK. Married couples fight sometimes, that's all. He shouldn't go off and leave you kids alone. I don't know what gets into him. But don't worry. He'll come home."

I wanted to tell her I wished he'd just go away, but I didn't. I could tell she wanted him to come back. I only said, "I can take care of Honey and me," and she hugged me again.

"I know," she said. "You're my good, big girl."

And that made me feel ashamed.

Mar needed Dad and loved him.

And I did, too. He was my dad. He *was* my dad, after all.

ON A SUNNY SATURDAY underneath the rhododendron bush, the air felt warm and steamy. As I crawled in and arranged the things I had brought with me, I could hear a robin scolding in the hedge. The wet of the ground seeped through the seat of my jeans, but I didn't mind. It was a warm wetness that went with the rich green smells and the humming, rustling, living sounds of the rhododendron bush.

Mary Rose and Daphne had gone shopping with their mother. Mar was at work. Dad had taken Honey to the doctor.

"You come, too," Honey had said, looking a little scared, but Dad had said, "You can stay home if you want to, Gil," and I was at an exciting place in my book, so I said, "You're a brave girl, Honey. You don't need me."

I was reading *Heidi*, and her world filled my head. Under the rhododendron bush, I had only to close my eyes, and I was in the Alpine meadow with Heidi and Peter, and the smells were the smells of wild flowers, and the sounds were the sounds of tinkling goat bells and the songs of the mountain birds.

I had brought a Swiss lunch to eat under the rhododendron bush, a lunch like Heidi and Peter ate—bread and cheese and milk poured into a bowl. *My* milk was cold from the frig, but I pretended it was warm like Heidi's milk, freshly squirted into my bowl from the udder of a goat.

I took a bite of bread and sipped my milk, the milk tasting strange and wonderful because I drank it from a bowl. If I felt a little guilty that I hadn't gone with Honey, I tried not to think of it. I picked up my book and held it so a ray of sunlight fell on the page. I began to read as I ate.

But the scolding bird was sounding more and more frantic. It was screeching and flopping from branch to branch. Suddenly it dived past me. Feathers and leaves and beating wings whirled in my face.

"Hey!" I yelled. I scrambled to my knees and covered my face with my hands. My book slid from my lap. My milk bowl overturned.

The bird thrashed its way back into the hedge. It shrieked.

"What in the world?" I said, and, "Oh, no!" My book was getting wet where it had fallen into the milk. I snatched it up and tried to wipe it off, but the wiping streaked the pages with dirt. My bread and cheese lay in a puddle of milky mud.

"You stupid bird," I said. "What's wrong with you?"

And then I saw the nest.

Kneeling, I could just see into it. She had built it in a fork of branches near the trunk of the rhododendron. It looked like a little mud-pie bowl, a-bristle with twigs. Inside, nestled in soft brown grass were four blue eggs.

"Oh," I said, suddenly understanding. "I'm sorry. I didn't know it was here."

The robin cocked her head and glared at me with a shiny black eye. Above the eye, like an eyebrow, was a white streak that gave her a look of surprise. "Tut-tut-tut," she chided.

I gathered up my things, leaving the soggy bread and cheese for the robin, and shook the last drops of milk from the bowl onto the ground. Then I backed out of the bush, crawling carefully, my eyes on the nest.

"It's OK," I said to her. "You can go back now. I won't bother you."

"Tut-tut-tut," complained the robin, hopping uncertainly toward the nest and then fluttering away again.

I stood up and looked at my ruined book. I wondered what the librarian would say when she saw it.

"Dumb bird," I said. "The rhododendron was *my* place, you know. Anyway, you've built your nest so close to the ground the cats will get your babies sure."

I shook out the pages of the book. Maybe if I wiped them with a damp cloth . . .

"Dumb bird," I muttered.

I heard the whir of her wings. The robin twittered contentedly as she settled on the nest.

"HONEY'S TAKING A NAP," Dad said. "Don't bother her." He was sitting at the kitchen table, shuffling through

some papers, and he kept his eyes on them as he spoke
to me.

"I won't," I said. "I just want my sweater."

"I said, don't bother her!"

I shrugged and turned around. I thought I had left my
jacket in the dining room. I could get it instead. But I felt
uneasy. As I passed the kitchen table, I thought Dad lifted
his head and looked at me. I could feel his eyes on my back,
a prickly feeling that made my feet hurry.

My jacket was on a chair. I picked it up and pulled
it on. Then I stopped and listened. There was a tiny little
sound. Did it come from our bedroom? I tiptoed across the
dining room and around the corner to the open hall door,
listening hard. Was Honey crying? I thought I could hear
Honey crying behind our tight-shut door.

"Gilly, what are you doing?" Dad's voice made me
jump.

"Nothing," I said. "I was just getting my jacket."

"Are you going, or aren't you?" he said.

"I'm going. I'm going right now."

Dad had told me to go to the store for some milk. The
money he had given me was clutched in my fist. I jammed
it into my pocket and headed for the front door.

"Be back in a minute," I called to him.

As I was going out, I thought I heard it again. The
tiny little crying sound.

CHAPTER ELEVEN

OMETHING was wrong with Honey.

Honey, who usually slept like a lump, quiet and heavy with warmth, had tossed and turned all night. She whimpered and flung her arms and legs about in her sleep, knocking against me and waking me up. Finally, when it was getting light, I got up and went to the kitchen. I poured a big bowl full of cereal and milk and took it back to her. Honey hadn't eaten much dinner last night. I thought maybe she was hungry. But Honey didn't want the cereal. She pushed it away, spilling some milk on the sheet, and burrowed down into our bed.

"Don't," she cried. "Go 'way."

She didn't even eat the breakfast Mar fixed later that Sunday morning. "Don't wan' it," she said when Mar tried to get her to eat her egg.

Now she was sitting on the floor in the corner, rocking to and fro and hugging her teddy bear. She was humming a tuneless little song. "Nony-nony-no," she hummed. She didn't want to hear a story. She didn't want to play. "No," she said. "Go 'way."

My stomach felt tight and sick. Something was wrong

with Honey, and I had an idea what. "You don't need me," I had told Honey yesterday. I had let her go alone with Dad to the doctor.

"Honey," I said. I scooted closer to her and tried to see her face. "Honey," I said. "Look at me."

But Honey buried her face against her teddy bear's head. She wouldn't look up.

"Honey, what's the matter?" I said. My heart was beating, big and scared, in my chest. "Honey?" I said. "Did something happen yesterday? Did something happen when you went to the doctor with Dad?"

Honey's voice was muffled against the brown plush of her teddy bear, but I think I heard what she said. I think she said, "He hurted my bottom."

"What?" I said. "What did you say?"

"He hurted me," Honey said.

"Who? Who hurt you, Honey? Was it Dad?"

But Honey just rocked back and forth, clutching her teddy bear.

I had to tell. I had to tell Mar. It was all my fault! I had to tell Mar.

I stumbled to my feet and ran from our bedroom. "Mar," I called. "Mar, where are you?"

"I'm in here, Gilly."

Mar had set up the ironing board next to the table in the dining room where she could see into the living room to watch TV as she ironed.

"Mar," I said, running to her. "Mar . . ." and then I stopped. Dad was in the living room, sitting in his chair with a book. He looked up, a frown on his face.

"What is it, Gilly?" Mar said. She was smoothing one of her uniforms onto the ironing board. "What do you want?"

"Uh . . ." I swallowed. I could feel Dad's eyes, looking hard at me. "Uh, I think Honey might be sick," I said.

Mar's smoothing hands paused over the white fabric of her uniform. She looked at me.

"She's acting funny," I said. "She won't play with me."

Mar walked around the ironing board and headed for the hall. I followed her.

"I think it's just her booster shot," she said. "Some kids react."

In our room, Mar knelt down by Honey and pulled her onto her lap. "What's the matter, chicken?" she said in her soothing, nurse's voice. "Still not feeling good?"

Honey nuzzled against Mar. "Nony-no," she whined.

Mar put her hand on Honey's forehead. She looked at me, and her face softened. "Don't look so worried, Gilly," she said. "She's just got a little fever, I think. It's a reaction to her shot yesterday."

I started to say, "No, Mar, it isn't that. It isn't her shot. It's something else."

But Mar stood up, lifting Honey in her arms. "Let's take a little nap, chicken," she said. "Let's take a nice little nap." She carried Honey to the bed. "Gilly, run to the bathroom and wet a cloth in cool water for me, will you?" she said.

"Mar—" I started, and then I turned and ran to do what she said.

By the time I got back, Mar had changed Honey into her nightie and tucked her into bed.

"Thanks, Gil," she said, taking the cloth from me. Slowly, softly, she wiped Honey's too-pink face with the cool cloth. She folded it into a little pad and laid it on Honey's forehead. "There now, that feels nice, doesn't it?" she crooned to Honey. "There now. There, there."

"Thank you, Gilly," Mar said, looking up as though she had just remembered me. "There's nothing more you can do. Don't worry. She'll be fine. Why don't you run along and play?"

I opened my mouth to say, "Mar . . ."

But she had turned back to Honey. "There now," she said softly. "There, there."

I COULD HEAR the sleepy twitter of the robin on her nest. She sounded like Mar, I thought. "Tut-tut," she said. There, there.

I couldn't crawl under the rhododendron without disturbing her. There was no place to go where I could think. And I *had* to think. I wandered back across the yard to the walnut tree, plopped down on the grass and put my forehead on my drawn-up knees. I had to think. I had to think about Honey . . . and the secret.

"Tut-tut," the mother robin twittered from the rhododendron bush.

First things first, I thought. Begin at the beginning and think it through. I closed my eyes and *tried* to think.

Yesterday, Dad had said, "You stay home, if you want to, Gil." Usually, Dad wanted me to go with him and Honey. Usually he said, "Take care of your sister, Gilly," or "Keep her quiet, will you?" Dad didn't like taking care of little kids. He was busy, or he was thinking about other things. "I've got things to think about," Dad said. "Important things."

Like the king . . .

When Juliana's father, the king, looked at her, his eyes saw something else. "Gold and jewels," he muttered. "Kingdoms to conquer. Dragons to slay."

It made Juliana sad.

Juliana embroidered satin slippers for her father's feet. She polished his crown 'til it shone like the sun. She went down to the kitchen cellars and cooked wondrous dishes to tempt the king. She plumped up the cushions on his throne.

And in the fullness of time, the king began to notice Juliana. He began to smile on her. At last, one evening, he called her to him, and filled with joy, Juliana answered.

Now it happened that a wicked magician had put a spell on the king. The moment the king touched his daughter, he was changed into a Beast.

When Juliana saw the Beast, she was filled with fear.

But there was no escaping, for the Beast spoke to her with the voice of the king . . .

I opened my eyes and gave my head a shake. That's make-believe, I told myself. That's make-believe. I need to think about what is real. I need to think about the secret. I need to think about Honey.

But *Juliana . . .* someone inside me said.

I got up and went to my flower bed. I knelt and began to smooth and pat the moist, dark earth with my hands.

Juliana . . .

The king was enchanted, but so was Juliana. When morning came, Juliana found herself whole and alive, waking from sleep in her very own bed. And her father was the king, not a beast, and his eyes were full of love.

But night after night, Juliana was called to the king. And night after night, the Beast awaited her. Juliana knew what would happen when she went to the king, but she feared to stay away.

And each morning she woke to the king's loving eyes.

CHAPTER TWELVE

 YANKED at a blade of grass that grew up through the clump of bluish-gray leaves at the end of my flower bed.

I need to think about me and my dad, I thought. Not about Juliana. Not about the king. I need to think about us and about Honey. About the secret.

The secret.

The secret happened because . . .

I wanted Dad to pay attention to me, I thought. And finally, he did. "You're changing," Dad had said. "You're getting to be a sexy girl."

Because I was sexy . . .

What's sexy? someone inside me cried.

You know, I thought. My hand jerked out and shattered the puffy head of a dandelion. The dandelion fluff floated vaguely away, settling on the clean dirt of my flower bed.

"No!" I cried out loud. I grabbed the ugly, naked stem of the dandelion and wrenched at it. The stem snapped off in my hand, but the leaves and roots gripped the ground obstinately.

"I don't *want* weeds here!" I said.

I don't want to, someone inside me was crying. I really don't want to.

But you did it, I told myself sternly. You did, whether you wanted to or not. You're not good and you're not beautiful and you make things up. You make Juliana up. You pretend and pretend, but you're not Juliana. You're not a princess. You are you—Gilly. Bad, ugly Gilly Harper, and it's all your fault!

"Whatcha doing?" Mary Rose said behind me.

I froze, trembling. Inside me, someone slipped away to hide.

"Whatcha doing?" Mary Rose said.

What was I doing? I looked at my dirty hands, sticky with dandelion blood. I watched my fingers open. I watched the stem fall from them. What *was* I doing?

"I was . . ."

"Guess what?" Mary Rose said. "Mom says, since we've got a school holiday tomorrow, you can stay overnight. Want to, Gilly? It'd be a lot of fun."

"I can't," I said. "I can't."

"Aw, Gilly, why not?"

"Because . . . because Honey's sick."

Mary Rose looked puzzled. "What's that got to do . . . ?"

"Oh, here you are, Gilly," Mar said, shoving open the back door. "Why, hello. Gilly, won't you introduce me to your friend?"

"Uh, yeah. Mar, this is Mary Rose Gibbs. Mary Rose, this is my mother."

"How do you do, Mary Rose," Mar said. "It's nice for Gilly to have a friend who lives so near."

"Hello, Mrs. Harper," Mary Rose said. "I just came over to see if Gilly could stay overnight at my house. My mom says it's OK if it's OK with you."

"Why, I think that would be lovely," Mar said.

They seemed to have forgotten *me* as they chatted back and forth so politely. I stood up and came over close to them and kicked the mud off my shoe against the bottom step.

Mar looked at me then. "Wouldn't that be fun, Gilly?" she said.

"I can't," I said. "Honey's sick."

Mary Rose's face was turning pink. She twisted her hands and looked at the ground. "It's OK if you don't want to," she mumbled, looking like she was going to cry.

"I'm sure she wants to, don't you, Gilly?" Mar said, a little too loudly. "Honey's just having a little reaction to her booster shot. There's nothing *you* can do for her, Gil."

"But, Dad . . . But, you have to go to work tonight," I stammered.

"I will tell Dad it's all right," Mar said, "and I'll be here tonight. I don't have to work until Tuesday."

"Oh," I said, and relief blazed inside me. I felt my mouth curving into a smile, and my hand that had felt so stiff and cold reached out and clasped Mary Rose's. "Oh, then . . . yeah . . . yeah, that would be fun, Mose. I'd *like* to stay overnight!"

"HEY," I said to Mary Rose. "Wanna see something?"

We were on our way to Mary Rose's house with my suitcase—really it was Mar's cosmetics case that she was letting me use.

"I found it yesterday," I said, setting the case beside the opening in the hedge. "Shhh." I put my finger to my lips and tiptoed to the rhododendron bush.

Mary Rose tiptoed after me, her eyes wide and wondering.

Carefully, I parted the thick leaves of the rhododendron and peered in.

The robin squawked in alarm and half rose, ruffling her feathers and shielding her nest with her outstretched wings.

I froze, and behind me, Mary Rose caught her breath. For a few thundering heartbeats, the robin glared at me from under her white eyebrow streaks. Then "Tut-tut-tut-tut-tut," she muttered and settled back onto her nest, preening her wings.

Slowly I reached behind me and drew Mary Rose forward until her face was beside mine, peering into the rhododendron bush.

"Oh," I felt her breathe.

I turned my eyes and grinned at her, and she grinned at me, her blue eyes bright.

The robin preened and muttered, watching us from the corner of her eye. "Tut-tut-tut," she said.

"THE TROUBLE IS," I said, "she's built her nest too low. As soon as the babies hatch, it'll be easy for a cat to get them."

We were sitting cross-legged on Mary Rose's bed.

Mary Rose looked worried. "Are you sure?" she said. "Maybe they won't find the nest. It's hidden pretty well."

I shook my head. There was a heaviness in my chest as I thought about it. "I guess you've never heard the racket baby birds make," I said.

Mary Rose picked at the little bumps on her pink dotted swiss bedspread. Her forehead was wrinkled in a frown. I saw her mouth set itself in a stubborn line. She looked up at me, and her voice was firm. "Well," she said, "we've just *got* to do something about it. We can't let them be eaten up by a horrid old cat!"

"Oh, Mose," I said. "There's nothing *we* can do."

Mary Rose jumped off the bed. "There *has* to be something," she said. "I'm gonna ask Dad."

"Mose . . . Mose!" I said, but Mary Rose had whisked through the bedroom doorway and disappeared.

"C'mon, Gilly," I heard her call. "Come *on*!"

Mary Rose's father was sitting in their living room. I could see the top of his blond head above the back of his chair. I could see the sections of newspaper he had tossed on the floor as he finished them, just the way my dad did.

I could hear Mary Rose chattering away about the robin and the endangered nest. And someone inside me was beginning, for no reason, to say, "Watch out. Watch out!"

Hesitantly I came into the room and edged around the chair until I could see Mary Rose. She was perched on her father's lap. Her hands were moving as rapidly as her voice, pantomiming the problem of the nest.

Mr. Gibbs listened quietly, his hand on her shoulder. They didn't seem to realize I was there.

I couldn't help watching. Watching for some little sign. The way he looked at her? The way he touched her? Watch out, Mary Rose, I wanted to say. Watch out! And I wondered if *this* was sexy—the way Mary Rose suddenly smiled and threw her arms around his neck and kissed him on the cheek? Mr. Gibbs hugged Mary Rose, and then I realized he was looking at me and holding out his hand. His blue eyes were warmly crinkled in a grin.

"Why don't we take a look in the morning?" he was saying. "Gilly, will you show me the nest tomorrow?"

My fingers tingled where Mr. Gibbs took hold of my hand and pulled me close to him and Mary Rose. Someone inside me was feeling scared. But it felt different—the quick warm way his big hand squeezed mine—different and nice.

CHAPTER THIRTEEN

AD WILL THINK of something," Mary Rose was saying, but her voice was muffled by the shirt she was pulling over her head.

I stood looking into Mar's cosmetics case while a panicky feeling whirled in my stomach. I hadn't thought about this when I said I'd stay all night. I was going to have to get undressed in front of Mary Rose! And then she would see—would see whatever mark the secret had left on me. I knew my body had to be different— dirty and ugly from what had been done to it. And Mary Rose would see and guess when she saw me undressed—would see I wasn't like other girls.

"What's the matter?" Mary Rose said. "Forget something?"

"Uh, no," I said.

Mary Rose had stepped out of her jeans. She pulled down her underpants. I tried not to look, but I couldn't help myself. She looked white and skinny, and her chest was flat, but I could see a pale fuzz of hair between her legs—just like me.

"Hurry up," Mary Rose said. She reached for a pair of yellow pajamas and began to pull them on. "I'm going to the bathroom before Daphne gets there first and monopolizes it," she said. "Get your 'jamas on and come quick. If she gets in there before we do, she'll be hours and hours!"

"OK," I said. "OK, I'll be right there." I began to unbutton my blouse. Saved, I thought, as she ran down the hall yelling, "Dibs on the bathroom! Dibs on the bathroom!"

I was into my nightie in the wink of an eye.

MARY ROSE'S VOICE was getting slower and softer, kind of blurry sounding. Running down, I thought, like a wind-up music box. In the middle of a word, Mary Rose yawned. I felt her turn over onto her side, warm in the bed beside me.

"I s'pose we should try to get some sleep," Mary Rose murmured.

"Yeah," I said.

It was quiet. I lay in the dark, next to Mary Rose, and thought how strange it felt to be in someone else's bed in someone else's house. The Gibbses' furnace came on with a rumble, and the sound startled me. It was different from the noise our furnace made, a deeper, steadier hum.

"Mose . . ." I said, whispering.

"Mmmm?"

"Mose, does your dad . . ."

"Mmmm?" Mary Rose murmured.

"Does he . . . ever do stuff to you . . . that you don't like?"

Mary Rose turned over again. "Sometimes," she said,

her voice sleepy. "Sometimes when I break the rules, he punishes me—gives me a job I don't like, or grounds me for a while. Why? Doesn't yours?" She yawned.

"Oh, yeah," I said. "Yeah, of course he does."

She didn't know what I meant. I felt relieved . . . but lonesome too somehow. It *was* only me. Only me . . . and then I remembered, and the remembering made my stomach sick.

Me and Honey.

MR. GIBBS'S FACE was sad and serious. He knelt beside the rhododendron bush and shook his head. Then he got up, brushing the knee of his pants, and beckoned to us to follow him back into the Gibbses' yard.

"I'm sorry, girls," he said. "I hoped you were exaggerating, but that poor silly bird has really gotten herself into trouble. The nest is way too low."

"Can't we put it up higher?" Mary Rose said.

"If we touch it, she won't come back to it," Mr. Gibbs said.

"Maybe the cats won't find it," Mary Rose said hopefully.

"I'm afraid Gilly is right about that, too," Mr. Gibbs said, and I hated being right when I saw the look on Mary Rose's face. "When they hatch out, the baby birds will make so much fuss, cats can't help but find them. I think this must be a young, inexperienced mother bird, who just didn't know any better than to build her nest in an impossible place."

Mr. Gibbs sat on their back steps, and Mary Rose plopped down beside him.

"But, Daddy," she wailed. "We *have* to do something!"

I hung back a little, watching as Mr. Gibbs put his arm around Mary Rose and gave her a squeeze. He patted the step on the other side of him and encouraged me with a look. Slowly, I came over to them and sat on the steps, being careful not to sit too close.

"Daddy!" Mary Rose said.

"Well," Mr. Gibbs said, "there *is* something, but you're not going to like what I think you should do."

"What?" said Mary Rose. "What, Daddy? I'll do anything."

"I think," said Mary Rose's father, "you should tear down the robin's nest."

"Tear it down?" I said, shocked; and Mary Rose wailed, "Daddy! Why?"

"Because, it's highly doubtful Mother Robin can raise a family in that location. But it's still early in the season. If something happens to her nest now, she has time to build another, perhaps in a better place, and lay more eggs. It would give her a chance to hatch some babies unmolested. And the babies would have a chance of growing up."

Mary Rose and I looked at each other. As if in response to Mr. Gibbs's suggestion, a cloud dimmed the sun, and I felt a cool breeze searching through my sweater.

"But, but the eggs . . ." Mary Rose almost whispered. "The eggs she already has . . ."

"I know," Mr. Gibbs said. "I know. I'm sorry, but that's the way it is. Sometimes painful things must be done to bring about happy endings. Sometimes, you have to take a chance. It may not help. But it's the only way for there to be even a possibility that Mother Robin can raise a family this year."

I swung my foot, kicking it against the step. Mary Rose twisted her hands in her lap. Her shoulders slumped.

"Don't look so gloomy," Mr. Gibbs said. "You don't have to do it. You can always just leave her where she is. If you hadn't stumbled across the nest, she'd have been on her own anyway."

Sometimes painful things must be done, I was thinking, and I was thinking of Mar, not of the mother bird.

"But it would make her so sad," Mary Rose was saying.

"Yes," said Mr. Gibbs. "For a while, she'd be hurt and angry and sad. She'd have to start all over. She'd have to work hard. But in the end, she'd probably be happy again, with a whole, safe nest full of little birds."

"It would be so cruel . . ." Mary Rose said, and her face and voice were thoughtful.

"It wouldn't be easy," Mr. Gibbs said.

Not easy, I thought. Not a bit easy.

"Think about it," Mr. Gibbs said. "You don't have to decide this minute. Right now, I think it must be time for breakfast."

He stood up and held out his hands to Mary Rose and me.

MARY ROSE sat on her bed, watching me pack my things into Mar's cosmetics case. I folded my nightie and yesterday's panties. I put in my toothbrush and comb.

"Maybe . . ." Mary Rose said ". . . maybe if we just left the nest alone . . ."

I closed the lid on the case and snapped the locks shut.

"Gilly, don't you think?"

I picked up the case and turned to face her.

"I've got to go now," I said. "Thank you for a very nice time."

"But, Gilly, we've got to decide!" said Mary Rose. "You can't go now!"

I shook my head. "I've got to," I said.

"You don't even care!" Mary Rose said, and her face got red. She jumped off the bed. "She's in *your* yard, and you don't even care!"

I walked across the bedroom and through the door. "Good-bye, Mary Rose," I said.

"Gilly!"

I turned around and looked at her.

Slowly, the redness faded from Mary Rose's face. "I

know," she said. "Dad's right. We ought to do it."

I saw her eyes fill with tears and felt my own eyelids prickle. "I'll help," I said.

THE MOTHER ROBIN screamed and squawked. As we lifted the nest out of the rhododendron bush, she scrambled frantically from branch to branch in the hedge above us, flailing her wings. Her eyes beneath their eyebrow streaks were wild.

"What'll we do with it?" Mary Rose said, cradling the little nest-bowl in her hands and staring at the four blue eggs. A tear splashed on one of them, making a patch of brilliance on the blue.

I shook my head. "Let's get it away from here," I said. "Maybe she'll calm down if we take it out of sight."

Mary Rose followed me toward my house. I carried Mar's cosmetics case. Mary Rose carried the nest. At the steps, I turned around and called to the squawking mother bird.

"I'm sorry, Mother Robin," I said. "I'm sorry."

"It's for the best," Mary Rose called. "You'll see."

Sometimes painful things . . . I thought. I wondered. I wondered if it really *would* be for the best.

CHAPTER FOURTEEN

THE HOUSE was quiet. There were no signs of breakfast in the kitchen. The living room was dark. I tiptoed across the hall to the closed door of our room and turned the knob.

Honey was sleeping on my side of the bed, the covers humped over her. I put Mar's case down and tiptoed to the bedside to look at her. Her face was pink and hot-looking, her hair curly-damp against her cheek. She breathed noisily through her mouth.

"Why, Gilly, are you home already?" Mar said softly from the doorway. "I was just coming to check on Honey. What time is it?"

I stepped away, so Mar could look at Honey. She put her hand on Honey's forehead.

"Poor little chick," she said.

I could see her mouth moving, but I couldn't hear the words for the pounding in my head. Tears were welling up and spilling on my cheeks. My stomach was tight. It hurt.

"Mar," I said, and as she turned to me, I knew how she must look, even though now I couldn't see her through my tears. "Mar," I said, "I've got to tell you something. Something bad. About Honey . . . and about me."

EVEN JULIANA deserted me then. I tried to picture Juliana dancing, and all I could see was Mar's staring eyes. I tried to imagine Juliana's music, and all I could hear was the gasp of Mar's breath—like I had hit her in the stomach, hard. Juliana was gone, and I couldn't escape in her. Juliana's goodness, her beauty, her happiness were gone. Taken away by Mar's voice—shrill beneath its quiet—Mar's voice in which I heard my badness, my ugliness, my hurt.

I wanted to stop it. I wanted to unsee what I saw in her face. I wanted to unhear what I heard in her voice. I was going to say, "Never mind, Mar. I made it up." And then I heard what *she* was saying.

"Are you sure, Gilly?" she was saying, over and over. "I don't believe it. I *can't* believe it! It isn't true!"

And suddenly I was mad.

"It is *too* true!" I yelled. "He did. And I didn't like it, but he said not to tell. And *you*, you never even noticed. You never even cared! You shouldn't have let him, Mar. You should have taken care of us!"

And then, at last, Mar was holding me—rocking me like a baby on her lap. For a moment, with the darkness of her shoulder shielding my face and her arms tight around me and her cheek against my head—for a moment, I was safe.

I THOUGHT I was telling for Honey, so Mar would make Dad stop hurting her. Later, I knew it was really for me. Because it wasn't right—what Dad was doing. Because I wanted it to stop for *me*.

Telling did that. It made it stop.

But I didn't want Dad to be mad at me.

He looked right at me and said, "I never laid a hand on her," and I was so scared, and so shocked, I couldn't say a thing.

I could see Mar hesitate. I could see she wanted to believe him.

"She's lying, Pat," Dad said. "I swear it."

Mar looked at Dad and then she looked at me, and her face was tight, and her throat worked. "I don't think she'd lie about a thing like this," she said. "I've never known *her* to lie."

I didn't want Dad to get as mad as he got then. I didn't want Dad and Mar to fight.

I didn't want Mar to be sad.

I didn't want to wake in the night in the crowded little room we shared at Aunt Ann's to hear Mar's crying. I didn't want her eyes to look dark and tired.

I didn't want to live with Aunt Ann.

"But *why* don't you live in your house anymore?" Mary Rose wanted to know.

And I didn't know what to say.

I didn't want Dad to stay away. Truly I didn't. When he wasn't living with us any more, I missed him, too.

"Where is Dad?" Honey kept wanting to know.

"He's at the house," I would say.

Honey would look puzzled and pout her mouth. "Then let's go home," she would say.

It got on my nerves, her always asking for Dad. It made me mad. I did it for you, I wanted to say. I told to save *you*.

But Honey hadn't needed to be saved.

"She meant the *doctor* hurt her bottom with the booster shot," Mar explained to me. Honey hadn't had a secret after all—probably just said what she did to impress me with what a big girl she was. I had made a mistake.

Not Honey! I thought exultantly, and then my stomach twisted, and my knees went soft. It *was* only me, I thought—something about me—that made Dad do it.

I didn't want to have to pretend that everything was just the same, when everything had changed.

I didn't want to wait, day after day, for the next bad thing.

I *didn't* want to tell anyone else.

I was scared when the policeman came. "Why do I have to talk to a policeman," I asked Mar. "Why does *he* have to know?"

"Because what your dad did was against the law," Mar said, "as well as being wrong."

"Will Dad have to go to jail?"

"I don't know, Gilly. I really don't. I just know we have to talk to the police—and be as honest as we can." Mar held her head with her hand, like it was too heavy for her neck to hold up all by itself.

"I'll tell him the truth," I said.

But, waiting for the policeman, it was hard to remember what the truth was. Had it really happened, or had I made it up? I do make things up, I thought. I made up Juliana. I made up the dancing garden. I made up the terrible Beast. I was turning the pages of my fairy tale book—a baby book I never looked at any more, but Mar had brought it from home with some of Honey's toys. A tiny folded square of paper fell into my lap. My hands shook as I unfolded it. I smoothed the folds and fitted the two pieces together. "Gillian," it said. "Gillian Harper. Pretty. Smart. Mysterius . . ." I remembered the day I brought home Mary Rose's books, the torn note treasured in my pocket. I remembered Dad, waiting for me on the couch . . .

I *hadn't* made that up.

Still, it was hard to remember all the things the policeman wanted to know. How many times? And when? And where?

"Will you send him to jail?" I asked.

The policeman ran his hands through his hair so it

stood on end in spiky tufts. "Gilly, I don't know," he said. "That depends a lot on your father." He wrinkled his forehead, and it seemed to me he was having to search for the right words, the way I had to search to find the words to say what Dad did. I wondered if he felt embarrassed, too. "The thing is," he said slowly, "it isn't your problem any more. Now it's my problem. I'll take care of it. Your father needs help, and I'll see that he gets it." He looked at me, and I could see his eyes were gray and kind. "You don't need to worry about it anymore," he said.

I didn't want to worry anymore.

I didn't want to feel so guilty.

I didn't want to feel so mad.

That's why Mar made me go see Mrs. Paul every week. "To help you with your feelings," Mar said.

Mrs. Paul was OK, I guess. I liked her big gypsy earrings and the way she looked right at me when she talked. But it bothered me—the way she kept asking questions, the way she kept saying, "How does that feel to you?"

And when I would say, "OK," she'd just keep saying, "How do you *really* feel?"

I didn't mean to tell her about Juliana. I don't even know why I did. But that was when I started to yell and couldn't seem to stop. That was when I hit Mrs. Paul and cried and cried and cried.

Because I *couldn't* make Dad stop all by myself. I had to tell. I had to tell!

But I didn't want it to be like this.

It wasn't fair—that I had to choose. It wasn't fair! It wasn't fair.

"It's OK to be angry when someone hurts you," Mrs. Paul said. "It's OK to be sad."

"Your dad is a grown-up, Gilly," Mrs. Paul said. "He should know what's right. He should know what's wrong. Grown-ups don't have the right to hurt kids, not even their own kids. Grown-ups don't have the right to make kids do wrong things. Your dad is mixed up. Perhaps it will help to understand that's why he molested you, but you mustn't blame yourself. The molesting was his fault, and all that has happened since is his fault, too."

Not my fault?

"Telling was the right thing to do," Mar said.

"The brave thing," said Mrs. Paul.

CHAPTER FIFTEEN

IT WAS SUMMER by the time we moved back to our house. Dad was gone, living across town. He was trying to get better, Mar said.

The day we moved, I helped Mar hang Honey's and my clothes back into our closet. I put my underwear and my socks back into our chest of drawers. I wandered out into the hallway, touching things.

Honey had turned on the TV in the living room. I felt my heart speed up when I saw the flickering, bluish light shining into the hall. I swallowed hard and made myself go through the doorway. Where Dad's chair used to be, there was an empty place. The carpet looked brighter there. Honey was dangling head down over the edge of the couch cushions, her legs against its back, watching TV upside down. She was humming to herself.

"Why don't you open the curtains, Honeybee?" I said. I ran to the window and pulled on the cord, letting in the light.

A book was on the table by the window. It was *Heidi*, the book I had been reading before we left. I picked it up and riffled through its dirt-stained pages. I couldn't remember the story. I would have to start over—after I paid the library fine.

I wandered into the dining room. I slid my hand along the backs of the chairs until I came to one that was pulled out from the table. I pushed it in.

In the kitchen, the counters were strangely tidy. The table was cleared. There weren't any dishes stacked in the sink. I pulled open the refrigerator door. In the bottom, way at the back, was a can of beer, lying on its side. Quickly, I closed the door.

The back door was locked. I turned the lock and pulled open the door. Through the screen, the yard looked sun-bright and warm after the dimness of the house. I pushed open the screen door and stepped outside, trying to see through the hedge.

I had not seen Mary Rose since school let out, weeks ago.

"Let me know as soon as you come home," she had said on the last day of school. "I miss you, Gilly. Please let me know."

"Mar," I called back into the house. "I'm going over to Mary Rose's for a minute. OK? I'll be right back."

Mar's voice sounded far away. "OK," she called.

I let the screen door slam behind me and started down the steps.

And then I saw my flower bed.

A tangle of round green leaves and brilliant blossoms

on curling stems spilled yellow and orange and red along the foundation of the house. My flowers had bloomed!

I ran back up the steps and flung open the door. "Mar," I called. "Mar, come quick. Come quick!"

Mar was in the doorway in an instant, her face drained white. "What is it?" Mar said. "Gilly, what is it?"

Speechless with wonder and pride, I could only point at my flowers.

Mar looked, and I saw the fright in her eyes wash away. She put her hand on her heart and sat down heavily on the top step. "Nasturtiums," she said.

"I pulled up the weeds to give the flowers room to grow," I said finally. "Look what they did."

Mar reached down to me and pulled me by my hand to sit beside her. She put her arm around my shoulders. Together, we looked at my flowers.

"I didn't mean to frighten you," I said. "I'm sorry, Mar."

But Mar only said, her voice husky-soft, "They remind me of Mother's garden, when I was a little girl." She squeezed me, and I looked up and saw her eyes—all shining—looking down at me.

"NOW," Mar said, after a little while, "why don't you go over and see if Mary Rose is home."

But Mary Rose was standing beside the opening in the hedge when I squeezed through, as if she was waiting for me. "Hi," she said, ducking her head shyly.

"Hi," I said, and after a minute, "I'm home." I was looking at Mary Rose's yard. The Gibbses' summer flowers were blooming too, and it was just as I had imagined it would be: a kingdom of flowers. A beautiful, tidy kingdom of flowers for Juliana, I thought. And then I corrected myself. For Daphne and Mary Rose. "Guess what?" I said. "My flowers bloomed."

Mary Rose smiled. "So did my rosebush," she said and grabbed my hand. "Come and see."

The roses were golden and small and fragrant.

"It *is* a Mary Rose-bush," I said.

Mary Rose was looking more like I remembered every minute. Her cheeks were pink with pleasure. "Gilly," she said. "Are we still friends?"

"Yes," I said. "Oh, yes!"

"Mom told us about your dad—that he doesn't live with you anymore," Mary Rose said. "I'm sorry."

I could feel myself blushing. I didn't know what to say. And then I remembered my talks with Mrs. Paul. "My dad has problems," I told Mary Rose. "He needs to work on them."

"Oh," said Mary Rose, and I knew she didn't understand.

"It's OK," I said. "We're OK, Mar and Honey and me." I thought of Mar's shining look. I thought of Honey, upside-down and humming, watching TV. "Really we are," I said. "We're getting along just fine." And even as I said it, I realized it was true.

"It's been lonesome without you," Mary Rose said. "Did you see your surprise?"

"Surprise?"

"In your flower bed."

"I saw my flowers blooming. I told you that."

"Yes, but did you see the special ones?"

I looked at Mary Rose.

She giggled and grabbed my hand, and together we went through the hedge.

"They're gillyflowers," Mary Rose said. "They were here all along, and we didn't even realize."

The spiky, bluish stems at the corner of the bed had bloomed, and the blooming had transformed them. In the clear, summer light, the stems and leaves were a soft, bluish-green. Silvery, I thought. And on each long, slender stem was a green-sheathed bud or small, fringe-petaled silken bloom. White, shining white, and streaked with red.

"Oh," I said.

"Smell," said Mary Rose. She dropped to her knees and buried her face in the blossoms.

I did the same.

The scent was warm and clean and spicy, like baking on a sunny day with kitchen windows open.

"Gillyflowers?" I said, wondering.

"You see, they make us kind of sisters," Mary Rose said. "Flower sisters, because of our names and because we each have a flower of our own."

"They were here all the time," I said.

Mary Rose laughed. "And we didn't even know," she said. "Until they bloomed, we didn't even know."

"We didn't even know," I said, and I found myself smiling.

In the walnut tree that shaded the corner of the yard, there was a terrific racket. I looked up just as a robin whirred over us and landed in the tree. She hopped from branch to branch, a worm dangling from her beak.

"Mose, look," I said, grabbing Mary Rose's arm. "Look there."

The robin hopped from branch to branch, high and higher in the tree.

Mary Rose and I shaded our eyes against the sun.

The robin hopped onto the edge of a nest, cradled among the leaves of a topmost branch. Five open, screeching beaks craned above the nest. The robin stuffed the worm into the nearest one. The other baby birds squawked and flustered. They snatched at the end of the worm as it disappeared into the lucky one's mouth. The mother bird stretched her wings and launched herself into the air, whooshing over our heads and into the rhododendron bush.

I looked at Mary Rose. Her mouth was open.

She looked at me. "Do you suppose . . . ?" Mary Rose breathed, and together we looked again toward the five jostling heads in the nest.

From the rhododendron bush, the robin trilled. I caught a glimpse of her—ruddy breast and smooth gray head and eyes black and bright beneath white eyebrow streaks—and then she took wing and soared over the hedge, the clear notes of her song rising with her.